"Don't thank me,"

Quincy warned Abby, covering her mouth with his hand when she opened it to speak.

"Why not?" she asked, her lips warm and soft against his palm.

"Because."

She turned her face to one side, and his hand fell to her shoulder. "Can I say one thing?" she asked.

"As long as it isn't 'thank you.'"

"You're not the big, bad guy you pretend to be."

"Yes I am," he said quietly. Why deny it? She was going to find out someday, anyway....

Dear Reader,

Celebration 1000! continues in May with more wonderful books by authors you've loved for years and so many of your new favorites!

Starting with . . . *The Best Is Yet To Be* by Tracy Sinclair. Bride-to-be Valentina Richardson finally meets Mr. Right. Too bad he's her fiancé's best friend!

Favorite author Marie Ferrarella brings us BABY'S CHOICE—an exciting new series where matchmaking babies bring their unsuspecting parents together!

The FABULOUS FATHERS continue with Derek Wolfe, a *Miracle Dad*. A fanciful and fun-filled romance from Toni Collins.

This month we're very pleased to present our *debut* author, Carolyn Zane, with her first book, *The Wife Next Door*. In this charming, madcap romance, neighbors David Barclay and Lauren Wills find that make-believe marriage can lead to the real thing!

Carol Grace brings us a romantic contest of wills in the *The Lady Wore Spurs*. And don't miss *Race to the Altar* by Patricia Thayer.

In June and July, look for more exciting Celebration 1000! books by Debbie Macomber, Elizabeth August, Annette Broadrick and Laurie Paige. We've planned this event for you, our wonderful readers. So, stake out your favorite easy chair and get ready to fall in love all over again with Silhouette Romance.

Happy reading!

Anne Canadeo
Senior Editor
Silhouette Romance

Please address questions and book requests to:
Reader Service
U.S.: P.O. Box 1325, Buffalo, NY 14269
Canadian: P.O. Box 1050, Niagara Falls, Ont. L2E 7G7

THE LADY WORE SPURS

Carol Grace

Silhouette

R O M A N C E™

Published by Silhouette Books

America's Publisher of Contemporary Romance

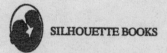

SILHOUETTE BOOKS

ISBN 0-373-19010-7

THE LADY WORE SPURS

CAROL GRACE

has always been interested in travel and living abroad. She spent her junior year in college in France and toured the world working on the hospital ship *Hope*. She and her husband spent the first year and a half of their marriage in Iran, where they both taught English. Then, with their toddler daughter, they lived in Algeria for two years.

Carol says that writing is another way of making her life exciting. Her office is an Airstream trailer parked behind her mountaintop home, which overlooks the Pacific Ocean and which she shares with her inventor husband, their daughter, who is now sixteen years old, and their eleven-year-old son.

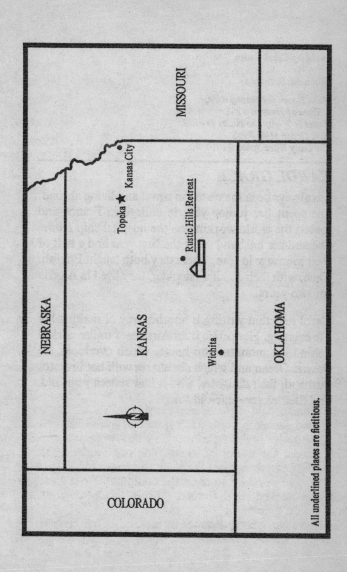

NEBRASKA

COLORADO

KANSAS

Topeka ★ ● Kansas City

Rustic Hills Retreat

● Wichita

MISSOURI

OKLAHOMA

N

All underlined places are fictitious.

Chapter One

Quincy McLoud drove slowly down the narrow road that bisected the prairies of central Kansas. Ahead, as far as he could see, was the tall green grass of the land he used to own. The land he'd worked and expected to live on forever. Memories came flooding back, along with a sense of loss so strong he felt empty inside.

He stopped his truck as he approached the boundaries of the ranch. There on a hilly pasture above him, where hundreds of cattle were grazing, was a woman driving along in her truck as if she didn't have a care in the world. Very likely the woman he'd come to see. He got out of his truck and watched while she honked her horn and waved her arms.

"Hooo-eee," she yelled out the window, her voice echoing across the waves of grass. The cows came running, crowding eagerly against the truck when she stopped in their midst. They pressed so close she couldn't get out to empty the hay stacked in the flatbed. "Shoo," she yelled, but the cows didn't move.

Even from a long distance he sensed her frustration. He could tell she didn't belong on a ranch, especially not on this ranch, and that encouraged him. Maybe she'd be willing to listen to reason once she understood the situation.

Impulsively he took the hill in long strides and, without speaking, unloaded the hay from the back of the truck while four women in designer jeans climbed out and eyed him with undisguised admiration. The cows meandered away from the truck to get to the hay and the driver opened the door and jumped down to face him.

"I suppose I ought to thank you," she sputtered, pink-cheeked and breathless.

He tilted his hat back on his head and studied her face. Wide blue eyes, no makeup, just a dusting of freckles across her cheeks and a sunburned nose. "I suppose so," he drawled, "but don't bother. It was my pleasure."

"It may have been your pleasure, but it was my job," she said, placing her hands on her hips. She had hair the color of golden wheat and wore it tied carelessly back in a pony-tail. But her eyes were as stormy as a Kansas sky in August.

"Sorry, ma'am, but it's hard to do your job when you're trapped inside your truck by a herd of cows."

"I wasn't trapped," she explained tersely. "I was allow-ing them to move at their own pace and not become agi-tated. Just using a little cow psychology," she added, while the four women followed the conversation by turning their heads from side to side.

Quincy's eyebrows shot up. So they were using psychol-ogy on cows.

Noting his surprise, she took a deep breath. "Thanks again, Mr...?"

"McLoud. Quincy McLoud." He held out his hand. Might as well start out on a friendly note.

She nodded and coolly shook his hand. "Abby Law-rence."

The name rang a bell, but he had to be sure. "You're the...?"

"Owner of the ranch."

Her handshake was firm, her palm sported a callus or two. So this was Abby Lawrence, the new owner of the Bar Z.

One of the women took advantage of the lull in the conversation to step forward. "You're the first, real, honest-to-goodness cowboy we've seen today," she said in a reverent tone.

"Really," he said as he looked them over. They seemed nice enough with their crisp, clean Western shirts and stiff, new leather boots. And maybe they were. It was the other woman who worried him. The woman who had what he wanted. "That makes us even," he countered. "You're the first cowgirls I've seen today. Where are the men?"

"This is Women's Week," Abby explained.

Quincy gave her an inquisitive look. Women's Week? What did that mean?

"At the Rustic Hills Retreat, we have a different theme every week," she explained.

And a different name, Quincy thought. His eyes wandered to the vast fields of tall grass. "Nice place you've got here."

"Thank you." A proud smile lighted her face as she surveyed the vast expanse of land. "I love it," she said simply.

"Love it?" he echoed, surprised at the passion in her voice. "How long have you been here?"

She tucked a strand of golden hair behind her ear. "About a year or so. I fell in love with this place the first time I saw it. Then I had to figure out how to pay for it."

Quincy noted the determined tilt of her chin, the full lips pressed tightly together. So it was love at first sight, was it? This wasn't going to be as easy as he'd hoped. She had a faraway look in her eyes that made him wonder where she'd gone. Suddenly she was back.

"Are you from around here?" she asked.

"Yep. I knew it when it was the Bar Z. A long time ago."

"Well, it was nice meeting you. We've got to be getting back."

Quincy's pulse raced. He couldn't let her get away so fast and yet he didn't know how to make her stay. "Just one thing," he said, stuffing his hands into his back pockets. "You don't really believe in love at first sight, do you?"

"It's happened to me only once, when I saw this land."

"Uh-huh."

"You're not a cynic, are you, Mr. McLoud?"

"Not me." Why *should* he be cynical? His wife had sold his ranch out from under him, and sent him a check for half the amount along with a copy of the divorce papers she'd filed. Maybe this woman did love the place, but not as much as he did, or even as much as his old foreman. "Pop still here?" he asked.

"You know Pop?"

"We're old friends."

"Come back and say hello before you leave," she said.

"I'll do that." He touched the tip of his hat and nodded to the women. "Ladies," he said, and loped down the hill to his truck.

Abby stood staring after him, vaguely aware that the women had jumped back into the flatbed and were trying to decide whether the cowboy looked more like a young Clint Eastwood or the Marlboro Man. Abby couldn't say. The only thing she recognized was his attitude. The "I can do anything better than you" attitude. She'd been married for five years to a man with an attitude just like that. It had been five years of feeling that nothing she did was ever quite good enough.

For five years she'd played the role of the perfect wife. Three years of mind-numbing office jobs while Grant finished law school, two years of being a corporate wife and all-round doormat while he rose to full partnership. And then, when he'd gotten to the top she'd found that she'd been playing her role all wrong.

As the wife of a law student, she was acceptable, but as the wife of a full partner, she didn't quite measure up. Something about the way she wore her hair, the way she didn't play bridge or shop at the right places, or didn't get pregnant on schedule to produce an heir.

Her ex-husband's new wife, his former secretary, would do better. She already had a head start on the pregnancy part. Bitter? To say that Abby was bitter was only part of it. She *was* bitter, but she had also been hurt, angry and completely devastated. It had taken her months to recover. But she had recovered and she wasn't about to let herself have a relapse. So the sooner Mr. Cynical left, the better.

She got back into her truck and started the engine. She had to get back to the ranch house with these women before the day was a total loss. They'd had trouble this morning giving the cows their shots, the cattle had spooked and broken a fence and the women had panicked. And now this. She'd planned to restore their confidence by letting them unload the truck and feed the cattle and then *he* had come along. The kind of man she was trying to avoid. Who was trying to help by doing her work and taking away her confidence. Not on purpose, of course. The man wasn't malicious. Just devilishly attractive and overly helpful.

After a bumpy ride back to the house, she saw he'd arrived ahead of them and was standing in front of the house staring at the front porch. If she hadn't noticed it before, she saw now that he *was* a real Western man, his body all angles and planes, his face shadowed by his broad-brimmed hat so that it was impossible to see the expression in his eyes.

She walked up to him, her hands in her pockets, wondering how the place looked to him. If he knew Pop, he'd probably been here before, and if he'd been here before he'd probably seen it in its heyday.

He stared at the sign over the door. "What does Rustic Hills Retreat mean? What are you retreating from?"

"*I'm* not retreating from anything. I'm offering people a retreat to the peace and quiet of the country, the solitude of the prairie, to a kind of renewal of the spirit...." She took a deep breath. Once she got started on the purpose of the ranch she had a lot to say, but one of the women interrupted her.

"We're going in for some coffee, okay?"

She nodded without taking her eyes from Quincy's sun-tanned face. "It looks a little run-down in spots," she said, following his gaze to the pen the cattle had broken through that morning. "But I have made improvements, a hot tub and ... would you like to see the new bunkhouse?"

"Why not?"

He walked with her to the two-story building behind the main house. He'd taken his hat off and the sun shone on his face, highlighting his straight nose, wide mouth and firm jaw. He was tall, towering over her five feet ten inches. She opened the door of the bunkhouse, wondering what he'd think of the new carpeting, the walls painted a pale yellow. Preceding him into the bunkhouse she told herself firmly that it didn't matter what he thought. She was on her own now, making her own decisions, subject to no one's approval.

"Is this where the ranch hands stay?"

"There are only two left, Rocky and Curly. They're out mending fences these days. We were losing cattle. But when they're here, they stay in the old blacksmith's cabin."

"How do you manage?"

"The guests do the work, or they will as soon as we get organized. You know how guest ranches work, don't you? We've been written up in several newspapers. I've even got a waiting list. Not everything works perfectly, of course...." She didn't mention the water heater breaking down, or the cook quitting, or the one woman who'd left before she'd even unpacked.

"Of course not," he said absently after a long silence during which his eyes took a tour of her body. Suddenly she was conscious of the smudges of dirt on her sweater and the tear in her jeans. She thought she saw a look in his eyes that said she wasn't up to the challenge. He wasn't the only one who thought that. But she'd show him and everyone else she could run this ranch and make a go of it.

She returned his scrutinizing look. He was attractive, if you liked the weather-beaten look, the eyes with a downward tilt, the spare frame that probably made women want to bake hot biscuits for him. He obviously belonged on a ranch, somewhere. Where, he hadn't said. He hadn't said much of anything. Just asked questions.

While she was studying his wide, expressive mouth and gray eyes, he reached out and removed a piece of hay caught in her hair. She gasped at the unexpected gesture. There was a strange look in his eyes. What was he thinking about? He snapped the piece of hay between his fingers, breaking the tension between them.

"Actually, I'm looking for a job," he said.

Her eyes widened. "Here?"

"Why not?"

"I told you there are only two hands and that's because I can't afford to hire any more. I wish I could." She didn't say that even if she could afford to hire someone, it wouldn't be him. He had too much of everything—looks, confidence and know-how. "If you want to work, you could try the other ranches around here. You shouldn't have any trouble. You seem able-bodied enough." That was putting it mildly. Yes, he was able-bodied, and then some. She wished he'd take his able body and head down the road. She didn't need this kind of a distraction and neither did the other women who were her guests this week.

"You've had experience?" she asked to fill the silence. Smooth, Abby. Did one ask Clint Eastwood if he'd had experience?

"Some. Sure you couldn't use me here?"

Her mouth fell open in disbelief. What did she have to do, spell it out for him? "I'm sorry," she said.

Sorry? She couldn't be more sorry than he was. She didn't know it, but she was sitting on his land. It wasn't her fault. She'd bought it from his ex-wife free and clear, not knowing it wasn't hers to sell. Oh, Corinne had had power of attorney. He'd given it to her when they'd called up the reserves for the Gulf War and he'd had to go. He'd been standing there in the middle of the Sahara Desert, the sun beating down on his head and the sand stinging his eyes when he'd got the check and the divorce papers.

"Well, thanks for the tour," he said. "I'll go say hello to Pop."

"You'll find him in the shed over by the barn. That's all his now." She held the screen door open for him and he turned toward the barn. She watched him go, relief flowing through her body like warm honey. She hadn't realized how tense he made her until he disappeared around the corner of the old building. She hoped he understood why she didn't have enough money to hire more help. If he knew anything about ranching, he'd know how hard it was to make it pay.

Her gaze drifted to the tall grass in the distance. Either people hated the prairie, thought its endless, tall, undulating grasses boring, or they read between the lines, finding beauty in the dense stands of bluestem, wild rye and prairie larkspur. She was in the latter group and she thought Quincy was, too. Fine, let him stay among the tall grass, but somewhere else, far enough so that she wouldn't run into him.

She turned abruptly and went to the kitchen entrance, banging the door closed behind her, unable to shake the image of his broad shoulders, narrow hips and long legs as he strode away from her. She had a ranch to run, guests to feed, and she couldn't afford a distraction.

The kitchen committee was waiting for her, three new arrivals from Chicago, oohing and aahing over the huge, old, cast-iron stove and the walk-in freezer with sides of beef hanging from hooks. This was what he didn't understand, the cowboy who knew everything, that with volunteers—guests who'd come to get in touch with nature—she didn't need a cook and so many ranch hands. That was not to say, however, that the women would be content to stay in the kitchen for very long.

"When do we learn to rope?" one of them asked, "and will it be from that big, tall hunk I saw outside?"

"We don't actually do much roping here," Abby explained, handing out bunches of spinach to wash and drain. "We move cattle in different ways. I'll explain it to you after dinner." She cracked fresh brown eggs into a bowl. "It's in my lecture on cow psychology."

"What about breaking wild horses?" a fresh-faced young woman asked eagerly. "Is that what he teaches?"

"No, he doesn't," Abby said firmly, cutting chunks of butter into the flour. "That man doesn't teach anything. Our horses have already been broken and they're ready to ride. Tomorrow we'll saddle up and round up the cattle for inoculations. But there are always regular chores to be done, too, like gathering eggs, putting out feed and mending fences. I'll pass out sign-up sheets later."

Abby was glad to see they looked reasonably enthused by the lineup of activities she proposed. She'd never advertised breaking horses or roping cattle. She didn't know where they got those ideas, probably from the movies, or from men like Quincy McLoud who looked like he could do them all with his eyes closed. She fluted the crusts in the glass pans and preheated the ovens. Then she looked out the window above the sink and wondered if he'd left yet.

Quincy rapped on the door to the shed and Pop yelled at him to come in. When the older man looked and saw who it was, he sprang from his cot in the corner with an exuberance that belied his age and his arthritis and pumped Quincy's hand enthusiastically.

"By God, I had a feeling in my bones you'd turn up one of these days," he said, his grin showing the gold tooth in the middle of his mouth.

"It's either your arthritis or ESP," Quincy said. "How are you doing?"

Pop waved his hand around the shed at the whitewashed walls and a new, extra large TV in a cabinet on the far wall. "Can't complain," he said. "Where ya been all this time, anyway? I been looking for ya ever since the war's been over. Shortest damn war I ever seen."

"Seemed long enough to me," Quincy remarked, taking his hat off. "I didn't exactly feel like coming back when it was over. Not after what happened. So I've been working for other people. Here and there. Until one day I couldn't take it anymore. Not until I at least saw the Bar Z again."

Not until he tried to get it back, he added silently. But then, no sense in saying anything to anyone about that. Not until he knew what he was up against.

"Well, it's not the same as it was, but I got a job, the lady says, as long as I want." He sat back down on the edge of the bed.

Quincy took a chair facing him. "What's she like?" he asked casually, as if he didn't know.

Pop grinned. "Like all women. Stubborn. What did you expect?"

Quincy nodded. That was exactly what he did expect.

"Didja meet her?"

"Sort of. How's she doing, anyway, without any hands but you and Rocky and Curly?"

"She ain't. The place is fallin' apart."

"And she doesn't notice?" Quincy asked with a frown. *He'd* noticed. It hurt him to see the sagging front porch, the kitchen garden gone to weeds and the broken fence.

"Nothin' she can do about it. She hasn't got the money to pay the extra boys. The way I heard it, she spent every last cent putting the down payment on the place and borrowed the rest. And she's determined to pay it off." Pop looked at Quincy. "Pretty little thing," he noted after a pause.

Quincy choked back a smile. The woman was a good five foot ten and Pop stood five-five in his well-worn boots.

"Don'tcha think?" Pop persisted.

"I didn't notice," he said. But he had. He'd noticed the way her chin had lifted proudly as she'd shown him her redecorated bunkhouse. He'd seen her blue eyes glow over her accomplishments. He'd felt the silky softness of her hair when he'd removed the piece of straw. Oh, yes, he'd noticed. He'd buried his feelings for women for so long he'd wondered if they were still alive. Now he knew. They were alive and well, too much so for his own good. He was anxious to get away from here, and yet he couldn't go. Not if he wanted a shot at getting the ranch back.

"Stay for supper?" Pop asked, reaching for his boots under the bed.

"I shouldn't," Quincy said cautiously. "She wouldn't like it." He stood and went to the door. Would it do any harm to just stay for supper? "Uh, I didn't tell her I used to own the place. So I'd appreciate your not mentioning it just yet."

Pop put his boots on and stood up. "She won't find out from me. And I'll warn Curly and Rocky. They'll be glad to see you. You can eat in the kitchen with me. Them guests eat in the dining room and talk nonstop. You know how women are. And I got some things to show you."

"Like the hot tub?" Quincy asked as they walked across the gravel driveway.

"Oh, you heard about that?" Pop chuckled. "Sure feels good on the joints."

Quincy stared at him. "You use that thing?"

"Doctor's orders. But only when the guests are having a meeting and the coast is clear. She said it was okay, Abby did."

They arrived at the back door just as Abby was lifting hot pans from the oven. Her face was flushed from the heat and wisps of hair had escaped from the rubber band holding her ponytail and curled around her face. She looked up and her eyes widened in surprise. The deep pie dishes wobbled in her hands. Quincy grabbed a clean bandanna from his pocket, took one pan and set it on the heavy wooden chopping block, then reached for the other. The smell of cheese and eggs made his stomach growl. He hadn't eaten anything since morning. He'd been apprehensive about coming here, coming home.

"Thanks," Abby said breathlessly, wiping her hands on her apron. She was surprised to see him, and it wasn't a happy surprise, he was sure. She'd probably thought he was long gone. And he would be if he had any sense. Or a home to go to. But all he had left was hope.

"This here's Quincy," Pop said to Abby. "Don't know if you two have met proper, but Quincy here is a cowhand.

And a damn good one, too," he said, slapping Quincy on the shoulder.

"So he said," Abby remarked, running her hand through her tousled hair. "I mean, he said he was a cowboy, he didn't say he was damned good," she amended.

Quincy watched her cheeks redden. She wasn't bad looking even when she was flustered, he thought, not bad at all. And she worked hard, feeding cattle during the day, or trying to at least, and cooking at night. Not many ranch women did both. Corinne had handled the books, period. She hadn't gone outside much, said the wind messed her hair and the grass made her sneeze. This woman's hair was a mess, all windblown and tangled, but she didn't seem to care. All she cared about was making a go of the ranch. Too bad she was going about it all wrong.

"I invited him to dinner," Pop explained, pointing to the built-in table and benches in the corner.

Quincy stared at the table, remembering having early morning coffee there before anyone was awake. Suddenly he was reminded of the fact that, once, he had had everything a man could want and that now he had nothing. He closed his eyes for a moment until the pain passed and opened them to find the two of them staring at him, waiting for an answer. But what was the question?

"I said, you're welcome to stay if you like quiche," Abby said.

Quiche on a ranch? First a hot tub and now quiche? What next, white wine?

"That would be fine," he said, removing his hat and hanging it on the rack next to the door as he'd done a hundred times or more.

She left one of the golden brown quiches on their table and took the others into the dining room. As the door swung closed, Quincy could hear high voices chattering and through the panel of glass in the door he caught a glimpse of women seated around the dining-room table. They'd hardly ever used it in the old days. That or the parlor. They'd seldom had company. Still he never thought he'd see it surrounded by women in well-pressed denims and bright shirts talking about how cute the cows were.

He took his seat across from Pop at the table and served himself a large helping of mixed green salad and a wedge of hot spinach quiche. He had to admit it wasn't that bad. It was just the idea of it he didn't like. People who worked on ranches were supposed to eat beef, and lots of it.

"So where ya off to?" Pop asked, cutting himself another slice.

"I'm not sure. Somewhere where they need somebody to run cows, mend fences, ride herd."

"Sounds like here," Pop noted.

"Nothing I'd like better than to stay here and try to get the ranch back somehow. But I asked if she'd hire me and she said she can't afford it. Hell, I'd work for nothing. I don't need the money. Besides, maybe one of these days she'll get tired of playing cowgirl and sell it back to me."

Pop held his fork in midair. "I don't know about that, but I know she needs all the help she can get right now. I can't really do much anymore. Still she lets me stay on for free. I been hoping she'd get somebody to take my place. You, for instance."

Quincy shook his head. "Not me. She made that perfectly clear. And maybe I couldn't take it, working for someone else on my own ranch."

"Better than hittin' the road again to God knows where. Man's got to settle down sometime."

"I *was* settled down," Quincy reminded him. "Then Desert Storm came along and unsettled everything."

"Give it a try," the old man insisted, getting up to pour himself a cup of coffee.

"I did, but she turned me down."

Pop held up a gnarled hand. "Leave it to me," he said in a stage whisper.

When Abby came back into the kitchen to refill the salad bowl, Pop was waiting for her.

"Can I talk to you?" he asked, holding the door to the refrigerator open for her.

"Now?"

"Just take a minute. I been thinkin' I ought to quit."

"Now, Pop, we've been through that. This is your home and I want you to stay as long as you want."

"Oh, I'm stayin'. I'm just not workin' anymore. Too old, too tired." Abby opened her mouth to protest, but he held his hand up to stop her. "Don't worry, I found somebody to take my place." His gaze landed on the man at the table. "Quincy, here."

They both spoke at once. "Wait a minute."

Pop turned to Abby again, who was still standing in front of the refrigerator with a head of lettuce in her hand. "You need help and Quincy needs a job."

"I can't afford—"

"He don't need money."

"There's no room—"

"He can stay with me."

"I don't want any—"

"More good-lookin' men around, I know. He'll just have to stay out of sight like I do." He grinned.

"Pop." Quincy cleared his throat loudly and they both turned to look at him. "The lady doesn't want me here, and I understand that. Anyway, I'm just passing through."

"Well let me know if you change your mind," Abby said with obvious relief.

"You could use some help," Quincy remarked, starting to warm to the idea. Maybe...

"Even if I did, it wouldn't work, you're not getting a salary."

"I'd only expect room and board."

There was a long silence. The voices in the dining room faded away as Quincy stared at the tall, shapely woman leaning awkwardly against the refrigerator door, holding an empty bowl in one hand, lettuce in the other. Pop stood motionless, speechless for once in his life, watching them watch each other, holding his breath. The tension increased with every passing moment. Quincy didn't move, afraid she'd say yes, afraid she'd say no. Who would make the first move? Who would break the silence?

A guest came banging through the door in search of Abby and the spell was broken. As Abby tore up the lettuce and tossed it in the bowl, she spoke. "It's okay with me if it's okay with him." Then she left without glancing at either of them and went back to the dining room.

Pop's eyes glowed with victory. He almost skipped across the floor to peer into the dining room through the window in the door. He turned to face Quincy with his back to the door. "She's not bad, that Abby," he said. "Just takes some gettin' to know."

Quincy rested his elbows on the table and stared at the tiles around the sink. Tiles he'd picked out and spread the grout between. Everywhere he looked there were memories—some good, some bad. How would it be to live among them, to bury the bad ones and keep the good? He could have said no. Maybe he should have. But if he had, he would have had to say goodbye to this place forever. Staying gave him a chance. Not a big chance, but the only one he had of maybe getting it back. The only way he knew of healing the wounds that had festered since that day he'd gotten his "Dear John" letter under the blazing desert sun. He'd bide his time and then offer to buy it back from her. And if that didn't work, he'd try something else. Because the ranch meant everything to him. It was his heritage, his birthright. Without it, he was nothing.

As for getting to know Abby, that was the first step. Because if he'd learned anything from the war, it was the importance of knowing your enemy. The enemy who occupied your territory. Then you could plan your attack. With Pop as his ally, he just might have a chance of getting it back. She'd said she loved it, but she couldn't possibly love it as much as he did.

After dinner Pop went back to his room to watch television and the women adjourned to the meeting room in the bunkhouse. Quincy filled his cup with coffee and wandered around in the dark. He didn't need any light to find his way. The familiar smell of grass came blowing across the prairie. He inhaled deeply as if he couldn't get enough of it. He'd been gone too long, been deprived of the sounds and smells he loved.

He'd almost forgotten how it seeped into your skin, became a part of you, the immense sky and the gentle hills. God, how he'd missed it. But what he really missed was a feeling of belonging. And he couldn't get that back until the ranch was his again. And that included his horse Magic, who was still in the same stall where he'd left him, still nervous, still high-strung, still raring to go.

"Tomorrow," he promised the stallion, reaching up to scratch the white diamond between his ears, "we'll go for a run. I promise."

After leaving the barn, he walked back to the bunkhouse and soon found himself outside the slightly open window looking in at Abby and the women in the meeting room. It had been the tack room in his time and now he hardly recognized it. She'd ripped everything out and started over. There was carpeting on the floor and there were folding chairs set up to face a podium with a blackboard behind it. Abby was standing at the blackboard drawing a picture of a cow with a circle around it labeled "flight zone." He shook his head. Flight zone? Where did they get this stuff?

She was explaining to the women that they could control the cattle by staying on the fringe of the flight zone. They leaned forward. They took notes and they asked questions. It was amazing to think you could learn to handle cattle by taking notes and listening to a lecture. He pressed his forehead against the window, a frown creasing his face.

At the same moment Abby looked up and met his gaze. Their eyes locked and held. Her cheeks reddened and she glared at him. He stepped back from the window. He'd made her mad. Had she sensed the disapproval he was feeling? He hoped not. He was trying to keep that under wraps. That was not the way to start out his campaign. He raised his hand in a mock salute, but she didn't see him. She'd turned her back to him and was facing the blackboard. But before he walked away, her words came floating out through the window.

"Cows are like people," she said. "You never know what they're going to do next."

"Amen," he muttered, and headed off into the dark.

Chapter Two

Abby went looking for Quincy first thing in the morning. The discussion of cow psychology had gone extremely well the night before. At least until she'd seen him peering in the window at her with a look of disapproval on his face. It was gratifying that the guests, at least, took her seriously. And now they were as ready as they could be for a full day's work.

Still, she hadn't slept well. Thoughts of Quincy McLoud had kept her awake for hours. Questions, doubts and fears. The first question was for herself. What on earth had possessed her to hire him? To take on a man who was willing to work for nothing. Why, when he was so obviously competent? Had she learned nothing from her past experiences? To remain strong and independent she must rely on herself alone. Had she allowed herself to be influenced by the look in his eyes, the look that told her what his lips never would—that for some reason he wanted to stay there more than he wanted to go elsewhere, but that he never asked for anything?

She was still bewildered as to how it came about. She went over their conversation in the kitchen, but it was a blur. If he didn't ask for the job, and she didn't offer, how had it happened, anyway?

Her boots made prints in the dry, brown earth as she made her way to the barn. The women were still asleep in the bunkhouse and the air was crisp and fresh. The sound of the wind in the grass soothed her jangled nerves, and she took a deep breath. A hawk swooped among the dense prairie larkspur and she followed it with her eyes until it flew out of sight. She didn't realize Quincy was standing there leaning against the barn door until she almost crashed into him.

Startled, she jumped back. He took off his hat and dipped his head. "Morning," he said.

"Good morning. I...thought we should have a talk."

"Sure," he said amiably. They walked around to the other side of the barn, where the early morning sun shone on two random bales of hay. She sat on one. He stood, propping his foot on the other. He was wearing a clean, blue denim work shirt, the exact color of the sky. Suddenly distracted, she wondered if he, too, had been savoring the solitude, the feeling of oneness with the earth, until she had come along....

She cleared her throat. However precious this time of day, it was fleeting fast and she had breakfast to cook, cows to inoculate, chickens to feed....

"Sorry about last night," he said, tilting his face toward the sun. "I didn't mean to be eavesdropping."

She felt the muscles in her neck tense at the mere memory of his face frowning at her from outside the window. "More likely you didn't mean to be *caught* eavesdropping."

"That, too," he admitted, a flash of humor in his gray eyes. "Is that how you learned about ranching, in a classroom?"

"As a matter of fact, I did take some courses from the extension and they were very helpful, especially the one in cow psychology." She studied his face to see if he was laughing at her, but not a sign of amusement crossed his expression. Reassured, she continued. "And I spent a summer at my uncle's ranch in Montana when I was young. I've never forgotten the fun, the freedom. Anyway... about today. You haven't changed your mind about working here?" She held her breath, not sure what she wanted to hear him say.

His gaze traveled the length of her stiff, new blue jeans to the tips of her leather boots, then slowly returned to her face. "Not unless you have."

She hesitated. The look he'd given her had her heart pounding. She was full of the doubts that had kept her awake last night. She'd changed her mind a dozen times and then changed it back again. And now in the clear light of day the answer wasn't any clearer than the day before. "There's a lot to be done," she said at last.

He nodded. "I thought I'd start on the fence." He gestured toward the pen the cattle had broken through the day before.

"Good idea." But it should have been her idea. She was the boss. She made the decisions. Not him. "And then..." she continued.

"Inoculations."

"That's for the guests to do."

"That's fine. I'll need all the help I can get."

"*You're* supposed to be helping *them.*"

"Sorry. I'm used to being in charge." He followed as she got up and walked into the barn.

A black stallion in the first stall reared up on his back legs and whinnied loudly. Quincy leaned in and reached his hand out.

"Watch out," she warned. "That's Magic. He's got a temper."

He nodded, and the horse came toward him with his head lowered. Quincy scratched him between the ears while Abby watched in amazement.

"How did you do that?" she asked. "I've been trying to ride him for months. He hasn't let me near him."

"I'm used to horses," he explained.

"So I see," she said dryly. She should have known. There wasn't anything the man couldn't do so far and he wasn't a bit modest about it. She backed out of the barn, her eyes on the horse she'd picked out for herself—once she got him under control. Then she looked at Quincy. "Breakfast's at eight," she said.

He shook his head. "If you want to get anything done, I suggest you get an earlier start. Say, five?"

"Five? Ask the guests to get up at five?"

He didn't answer. His attention was on the horse. He spoke to it softly, then turned back to her. "Mind if I saddle him up?"

She shrugged. "Be my guest." But if he were a guest she'd tell him he couldn't ride the horse. The difference was he was an employee, an employee who didn't get a salary. She was beginning to think it was a terrible combination. Before she left the barn she saw him throw the saddle over Magic and then she turned back to the kitchen. So he wouldn't listen to her. Let him get himself thrown off. Let him learn the hard way.

The next time she saw Quincy was after breakfast in the corral. She had mustered most of the twelve women who'd paid for the privilege of doing chores on a working ranch for a week. They'd come to escape the pressures of job and family, here for a break in their routine, whatever it was, and it was up to her to send them back with a feeling of accomplishment, a feeling of success.

She'd saddled a horse for each of them, giving them a leg up when needed, and taken one of the leftover horses for herself, an old roan named Jessie. Out of the corner of her eye, through the red dust stirred by the cattle milling and mooing and stomping their hooves, she saw Quincy approaching on Magic, looking like he belonged there. She turned her eyes to the women, watching them gamely weave their way through the tightly packed cattle.

A feeling of pride welled up in her chest. Over the noise of the cows bellowing, Abby shouted as Quincy grew closer. "Do you believe," she called, "that most of these women have never ridden before and none of them have ever handled beef except at the supermarket?"

"I don't believe it," he said.

Her eyes searched his face, trying to decide if he was being sarcastic, but there wasn't time. The cows were edgy, restless, and had to be brought into a single line before entering the chute. Despite her lecture, the women had forgotten that cows like to keep their handlers in sight. And when they couldn't, when you were right behind them, it made them veer unpredictably to either side, trying to see you.

Quincy frowned. "Did you tell them the cattle should be in a straight line?" he asked, watching the women shout and wave their arms.

"I explained it to the women, but not the cows," she said pointedly. Everyone knew cattle were unpredictable, even if you did everything right.

"Maybe that's the problem," he muttered. "Is this everybody?" He gestured toward the women.

"Most everybody," she said, tightening her hold on the reins. "Some of the women aren't scheduled to help with the cattle today and chose to stay in the bunkhouse and read," she explained.

"About the role of women in the settling of the West?" he asked.

"Among other things. I know what you're thinking. That in your day ranch hands never took the day off to read. Well, maybe they should have. And don't forget, they were getting paid. These women are paying me. They're my guests."

"That's not what I was thinking," he said. "I was thinking we ought to get started. If you're ready."

"Of course."

Without another word, Quincy rode off to open the headgates and the chute doors. She didn't remember assigning him that job, but he was doing it. She did remember telling the women not to hoot or holler at the cows, but they couldn't resist, and the cattle were balking, refusing to enter the solid, curved chute. Maybe they knew they'd be stuck with a needle at the other end and they were having no part of it. But Abby had ordered the chute built according to the rules—high enough so the cows couldn't see over the sides—and they wouldn't know what was at the other end until they were almost there.

When the cows finally started moving steadily in a straight line, thanks to Quincy's skillful maneuvering, Abby dismounted and went back to see how the shots were going.

"That's good," she said, watching an eager librarian from Kansas City jab the needle into the cow's hindquarters.

The woman grinned happily. "It's not quite like practice where you had us poking the oranges," she told Abby, "but I think I've got the hang of it now."

Abby nodded her approval and went back to the corral just in time to see Louise, one of the women who'd been eyeing Quincy with frank admiration, being carried off out of the corral and into the fields on Scout, one of the younger, spirited geldings. Louise was screaming, her face contorted as she raced by, her hands clamped onto the saddle instead of the reins.

Her heart pounding, Abby jumped onto Jessie and headed after her. She remembered specifically that Louise had told her she could ride anything. Abby urged Jessie on, but she was old and tired and didn't see what the rush was about. A blur of blue denim and red-brown horseflesh shot past her and Abby knew it was Quincy. They moved like one, the tall, lean man and the horse with its mane flying in the wind.

By the time Abby caught up with them, Quincy had brought Scout under control, had transferred Louise onto his horse and she was looking like there was nowhere else she'd rather be. Guilt, mixed with resentment and relief, flooded Abby's body.

"What happened?" she asked Louise, pulling up along-side Quincy and the shaken woman.

Louise opened her eyes as wide as she could. "He saved me," she said, looking at Quincy adoringly.

"I see that," Abby said. "I mean, what made her bolt like that?"

Louise shrugged helplessly and leaned back against Quincy's chest. To his credit, he looked distinctly uncomfortable. It was a little late for discomfort, she thought disgustedly, *after* he'd made his heroic rescue. Louise looked like she was attached to him with glue. Not that it mattered, except that this was supposed to be a learning experience and how could anyone grow and learn when they were leaning on a man who could ride, rope and corral cows better than any of them? Maybe this wasn't going to work, after all, having a macho cowboy around all the time, racing to the rescue when things went wrong. There would always be incidents and the guests would never learn anything while Quincy was around. Especially if they were to follow Louise's example, melting all over him. So what if he was gorgeous?

No, even if he didn't cost her any money, Quincy's presence would cost her her goal. Her goal of helping others achieve their potential, learning by doing.

"What made her bolt was that the cows panicked," Quincy explained. "And what made the cows panic was that one of the ladies sitting on the fence was flapping her red jacket around."

Abby squeezed her eyes shut for a second. She'd carefully explained about sudden movements and bright colors. She knew it was in the handout. "Panicked!" she asked. "Are the cows still panicked?"

"Very likely," Quincy answered, and took off with an excited Louise sitting in front of him. He dumped her at the entrance to the corral and by the time Abby caught up with him, he'd calmed the cattle and had them lined up in a single file waiting for their shots at the end of the chute.

"There's some hangup back there with the shots," he told Abby. "Go back and see what it is while I keep them coming."

Out of the corner of her eye Abby saw the other women, still on horseback, look from Abby to Quincy, sensing an argument coming.

She took a deep breath. "That won't be necessary. The women will keep them coming. You can go back to repairing the fence."

It only took him a second to recover from the shock of being ordered to do something by anyone else, let alone a woman. Abby was sure she was the only one who noticed the brief tightening of the muscles around his mouth before he turned without a word and rode off to the pasture to repair the fence. She exhaled a shaky breath. She'd passed a hurdle. She'd told him what to do and he'd done it. She'd taken control of the operation. The women looked at her with what she perceived to be new respect, or was it disbelief? Why would anyone order Quincy McLoud away from the action when he was so obviously qualified to take charge? So obviously experienced and so obviously looking like a cowboy right out of a Universal studio?

That was the last time she saw Quincy all day and, coincidentally, the last time anything went right all day. It was just a coincidence, she told herself. She didn't need him to make things work, it was just one of those days. One of those days when the guests barely made it through the morning with their confidence intact. Needles broke, cows slowed and horses balked.

In the afternoon, instead of returning to the corral and the animals that needed inoculating, the guests chose to do other less demanding chores like feeding the chickens and collecting eggs. Which was fine. It was their choice. But inoculating all by herself was impossible. If Pop hadn't come by to help her, she couldn't have done it.

Hauling a stool from the barn, he took over giving shots from Mary Beth, who'd been at it all morning.

"Why didn't ya tell me ya needed help?" he asked, frowning up at Abby.

"Your doctor told you no hard work."

"This ain't hard," he said, slapping the cow on the rump after he'd shot her full of immunities to hoof-and-mouth disease.

"They thought so," she said, watching the women round the corner of the barn on their way to the henhouse.

"Well, sure they did, but they also thought it was a hell of a good time," he said.

"They did?" She leaned against the fence, not realizing how hungry she was for an encouraging word, however small or insignificant.

"Yup. I heard 'em at lunch. Said they'd never forget it."

"Is that good?"

"Course it is. Speaking of lunch, I never saw Quincy come in. Where is he?"

"Mending fences," she said, looking out toward the pasture. When she'd asked him—no, *told* him—to go, she hadn't meant for him to stay there, nonstop, without a break for lunch.

"Mending fences?" Pop said. "If he was here where we need him we'd be done by now. He can shoot cattle down a pen faster than anybody I know. The cows respect him."

Abby held her chin high. "That's the trouble. Everyone respects him. Too much. When he's around, the guests feel intimidated. I do, too. I was afraid of this. And he's only been here one day."

Pop gave her a sharp look. "He's a good man," he said, "or I wouldn't have suggested you hire him."

"I know you wouldn't, but . . ."

"Proud, too."

"He has a right to be proud," Abby agreed. "He's good at what he does."

"And he's crazy about the land," Pop added. "He loves the land more than anything, so don't worry none about him flirting with the guests, cause no woman can compete with the strong feelings he's got for the Flint Hills."

"I'm more worried about them flirting with *him,*" Abby said, rubbing her hand across her forehead.

Things went smoothly with Abby on one end of the line of cattle and Pop on the other until she discovered that Pop's elbow was swelling. He said it was a sign of a change in the weather, but she said it was a sign of his osteoarthritis acting up and ordered him to the tub for a hot soak and to bed.

Since it was already five o'clock, she separated the cattle who hadn't been inoculated from those who had and then went to the kitchen to grate cheese for eggplant parmigiana. A loud thump and a sharp splintering sound from the front of the house startled her. She dropped the grater on the floor and shreds of cheese flew in all directions. Racing outside, she saw that her truck had been backed into the power pole and, as she watched in horrified silence, the last phone lines snapped and the pole came crashing to the ground.

Melissa and Brenda, two sisters from Cleveland, got out of the truck looking shocked and chagrined. "Oh, Abby, I'm so sorry." Melissa's eyes filled with remorseful tears.

Abby walked slowly toward the truck, telling herself to be glad it didn't have anything worse than a dented fender and that no one was hurt. But with the lines down, they were now without electricity as well as a telephone.

"Don't worry," she said soothingly, her mind already racing for a solution. "Just stay away from the whole mess. Especially the power lines. Let them lie there until I call... Never mind, just leave everything the way it is."

"We wanted to surprise you by taking the hay out by ourselves," Brenda said.

"You did surprise me," Abby said with a quick smile, although she was fighting off a sick feeling in the pit of her stomach. She could just imagine what Quincy would say when he saw what happened. He already had a low opinion of the guests on guest ranches. As if these things never happened to ordinary people. As if they never ran into anything.

They'd have to get the generator going right away. It would be days before the power company would get there, especially if they couldn't call them on the phone to report the damage. In the meantime they had to keep the pump running before they used up all the water in the storage tank. If the pump lost its prime they'd have a real problem. They could get along without lights, and the cookstove ran on propane, but they couldn't do without water.

Pop knew how to start the generator. He'd promised to show her, but hadn't had a chance to yet. And she couldn't ask him to get out of bed now. Quickly she saddled Jessie and went out looking for Quincy. She'd been seriously thinking about letting him go, he was a distraction, no matter how knowledgeable, to the guests and their host, but could she really ask him to start the generator and then fire him? Could she fire him at all when he worked for nothing? Was it possible to fire a volunteer?

When she found him, he was winding wire around a post with his shirtsleeves rolled above the elbows, the muscles in his forearms straining. The sun was behind him, backlighting his powerful upper torso. She caught her breath at the sight of his raw strength. He was so intensely involved in his work, he didn't see or hear her coming until she'd dismounted. Then he looked up and watched her approach, measuring her steps with all the easy assurance of a man who knew he was indispensable. She had half a mind to fire him right then and there, but dammit, he *was* indispensable. Especially now.

"You missed lunch," she said by way of a greeting.

He looked up at the white clouds scudding across the sky. "I thought I'd get this done. Before I leave."

She stopped dead in her tracks. "Leave?" Funny, all the time she'd spent thinking about firing him, it had never occurred to her he'd quit first. How could he quit when he'd just started, and why?

He set the roll of wire fencing down next to the post and gave her a long look. "I don't think it's going to work out, you and me."

"Because you don't like to take orders," she suggested.

"Because *you* don't like to take suggestions," he countered.

She walked closer, her hands on her hips. "I've been taking suggestions all my life, some good and some bad. I think I can tell the difference between them by now."

"And I took enough orders while I was in the reserves to last me a lifetime," he said, hooking his thumbs in the pockets of his faded jeans. Had the guests noticed how they molded to his legs like a second skin? No wonder they forgot their instructions. No wonder they couldn't concentrate on cattle with him around.

"I suppose not one of those orders came from a woman," she said.

"That has nothing to do with anything. I like women. Except for my ex-wife, I have no problem with women. Can you say the same about men?"

She felt the color rise to her face. "Of course, I can. Just because I've set aside one week for women on my ranch doesn't mean I don't like men. I was married to one."

"I see," he said. "What happened?"

She tensed. He had no right to pry into her personal life. And she had no obligation to answer such a question, but for some reason she felt it important to do so. "He wanted a divorce so he could marry someone else," she said. There, it was out. And just reducing it to words made the whole episode fade a little in significance.

"Would you do it again?" he asked.

"Never," she said.

"Neither would I."

They stared at each other, locked for a brief moment of mutual understanding. But it couldn't last.

"Is it too much to ask that on my ranch you do what I say?" she asked.

"As long as your guests do what you say, too. As long as we're all working together and not at cross-purposes." He twisted a stub of wire around his finger.

"There's a difference. They don't work for me."

"Agreed. But you don't need guests. You need ranch hands. Men—or women—" he added, "who know what they're doing. Otherwise you'll never make it. You've got cows out there who need their shots, unless you finished to-day...."

She shook her head. He knew they wouldn't finish, not without him. She kept her eyes on the curved line where the sky met the hills in the distance. "Maybe I shouldn't have sent Rocky and Curly out to mend fences right now, but..."

"You've got calving coming up and then weaning later on. Have you ever done it before?"

"Not yet."

"It's a twenty-six-hour-a-day job for everyone. Can you ask your guests to do that?"

"I'll ask them to help," she said. "And I'll ask you, too."

He met her troubled gaze and then let his eyes roam over her body from her checkered shirt to the tips of her dusty boots. She was long and tall, with curves in all the right places like that blond model he'd seen pictures of with the pouty lips. Not that Abby pouted. She came right out and said what was on her mind. He liked that about her. Was that why he was considering staying to help her through the rough times ahead, because he liked her?

It wasn't for her, he assured himself. It was for the ranch. He couldn't stand by and watch it go down the tubes. He doubted very much whether she or her guests could make it through calving or weaning and still want to come back for more. So what was the problem? Why should he worry? Once she realized she couldn't make it, she'd have to sell and he'd be the first in line with an offer she couldn't refuse. For the same amount she'd paid for it, he'd buy it back. Yes, all he had to do was be patient, and he'd have what he wanted.

He nodded. "All right," he said finally.

She exhaled slowly. "If you're staying, would you mind starting the generator for me? The power went out. I'd ask Pop, but he's had an attack of his arthritis and I don't want to bother him."

Quincy said he would and then he untied Magic from the post where the stallion had been chewing grass. He held out the reins and put them in Abby's hands. He'd seen the longing in her eyes when he'd ridden by her this morning. Maybe she'd appreciate his horse as much as he did, but whether she did or didn't, she deserved a chance. She looked at him, her eyes darkening in surprise.

She took the reins with only a slight hesitation, then mounted the horse quickly with surprising grace. Whenever, wherever, she'd learned to ride, it wasn't yesterday. Magic whinnied and tossed his head. Traitor, Quincy thought, as he mounted the old roan. But he watched admiringly as Abby trotted ahead of him on his horse, back straight, head held high, blond hair blowing in the wind. Then with a burst of speed old Jessie didn't know she had in her, Quincy caught up with her. And they rode together without speaking, back to the ranch.

Together they went straight to the generator, which was where it had always been, in the storage shed behind the barn. The door was wedged shut, as if it hadn't been opened since he'd left. He put his shoulder against the door and shoved it open. An earthy, musty smell greeted him. With Abby right behind him, he shone his flashlight around the interior, noting the hard-dirt floor and a network of spiderwebs hanging from the ceiling. A tight feeling of unreasonable fear coiled deep in his gut. Spiders terrified him more than the sound of a Scud missile. But this wasn't a Black Widow, like the insect that had bit him when he was a child, so what was the big deal? He closed the door quickly and leaned against the outside of it. He'd go back in a minute, as soon as his heart stopped pounding.

"Anything wrong?" Abby said, watching his face.

"You ought to learn to do this yourself, in case nobody's around the next time," he spoke quickly, diverting her attention. "By the way, what did you say happened to the lines?"

"You haven't been around to the front of the house?"

He shook his head.

"There was an, um, accident involving my truck and the power pole."

"Who was driving?" he asked with a frown.

"One of the guests. I'll go to town tomorrow to notify the power company. The phone's out, too, of course. In the meantime..."

"You're not afraid of spiders, are you?" he asked abruptly.

"Of course not."

"Then you can start your lesson by removing the spider or spiders who's taken up residence in there."

Hiding a smile at Mr. Cynical's suddenly pale face, Abby decided not to comment. She merely opened the door and reached in her back pocket for her handkerchief.

He watched while she picked the lone spider up and deposited it outside. He didn't know women still used handkerchiefs and he didn't know women who weren't afraid of spiders, either. Nor had he ever thought he'd come across one who wouldn't die before *not* asking nosy questions. There was a first time for everything.

"Now," he said when they were both inside the shed, the door closed behind them, "see that valve under the gas tank?"

She stepped past him and crouched down in front of the two-foot-high, four-hundred-pound generator and suddenly the musty smell was replaced by the smell of flowers that wafted toward him from her hair. He bent over, inhaled deeply, then took her hand and placed it on the knob under the fuel line.

"There. Turn it, like this." Together they turned the knob. Her shoulders brushed against his chest and he struggled to keep his balance. It wasn't easy given the tight quarters and the smell of her hair invading his senses. "Now, close the choke. The little lever on the carburetor. You do know what the carburetor is, don't you?" he asked, his face so close to her he could feel her hair brush his cheek. He rocked back on his heels.

"Of course," she answered breathlessly.

To be sure, he took her hand and guided it forward until she found it. Then he pulled her up by the elbows, her back to him. "Take the starter cord and pull. And I mean, really pull." He backed up as much as he could in the small room and braced himself. But she pulled so hard she reeled, fell against him and sent them both sprawling backward onto the floor.

Quincy nearly groaned out loud. They couldn't have been closer if he'd pulled her back to sit on his lap on purpose. Her bottom was cradled against his knees. There was a moment of stunned silence where neither of them breathed. He could feel the warmth of her body through her cotton shirt and tight jeans. The sweet fragrance of her almost overwhelmed him.

"You told me to pull," she reminded him at last.

"And you did," he assured her, doing his best to bring his breathing back to normal. "Next time...try to hold on...to the cord."

She braced her hands on the dirt floor and got back to her feet. But for some reason he stayed on the floor, staring up at her, temporarily unable to move a muscle. She held her hand out and he took it and let her pull him to his feet. Normally he would have grabbed the starter impatiently and finished the job. But this was not a normal situation. Being alone with a woman in the shed was strange enough. Having her body flung against his and landing on the floor with her every curve meshed against his was downright disturbing. He continued to hold her hand and stare at her.

Instead of his customary impatience, a strange calm had settled over him. He was prepared to wait until she started the motor herself if it took all day and, all things considered, it just might.

"Pull it harder this time," he insisted. "You can do it."

She bit her lip, and she squared her shoulders for yet another try. Over and over she pulled on the cord only to have it fall limply in front of her. But she didn't quit. She kept yanking on the cord, her face getting redder every minute. And finally, just as he thought she would have to give up, the engine roared to life. Elated, she spun around to face him.

"I did it," she crowed, throwing her arms around him.

It took all his willpower not to crush her to him, to feel her body against his, to share her elation and success in a different way. Instead he held his arms at his sides and closed his eyes to avoid the sparkle in her eyes and the dazzle of her smile.

"Not bad," he said, running his hands down her arms to make sure she hadn't strained a muscle yanking on the cord for so long.

"Not bad?" she asked, looking up at him. "Is that all you can say?"

Something went still inside him. His hands cupped her elbows. Her arms were linked loosely around his waist, and her face was tilted up to his, her lips upturned, smiling triumphantly, inviting him to share her success. It crossed his mind that if he kissed her now no one would know, not Pop, not the guests. It was just the two of them, and something told him she might not mind.

"It took you long enough," he muttered, but he could feel the corners of his mouth quirk into a half smile.

"That was to make you feel good. If I'd done it right the first time you wouldn't have felt useful, would you?" she teased.

"Feeling useful is not what I'm aiming for."

"What is?" she asked, suddenly serious.

He almost told her then. He almost said, *Getting my ranch back is what I'm aiming at. Is* all *I'm aiming for.* But he couldn't say that. So instead he said, "To help you out. To pass the time until . . . I move on."

She dropped her arms to her sides as if she'd forgotten how they got wound around him. She brushed her hands against her jeans and looked around as if she didn't know where she was. For some reason he felt a peculiar sense of loss now that she wasn't sparkling at him. What was wrong with him?

"Well," she said resting her hand against the door, "if you have any more trouble with spiders . . ."

"I'll give you a call," he said. Sure he would. From now on he would avoid coming in contact with spiders *or* women. Experience told him he didn't get along with either.

Then why did he continue to stand there in the middle of extremely close quarters with a very attractive woman and God only knew how many spiders? Because he was enjoying himself, he realized with a start. Because he liked looking at her and he liked listening to her, even though he didn't like what she was doing to his ranch. He put his hand next to hers on the door, his palm flat against the rough wood, but neither of them pushed against the door to open it.

"You're not really afraid of them, are you?" she asked softly.

"Only the dangerous kind," he said, moving his hand until his fingers brushed against hers. The tips of her fingers trembled just slightly. Her eyelids flickered a warning. And he knew why. Not all spiders were dangerous and neither were all women, but here was one who could cause him trouble. Who'd already come between him and his ranch. What was he doing? He'd been about to— Cursing inwardly, he pushed against the door and a gust of fresh air rushed in and blew away the cobwebs. No more webs, no more spiders, just one dangerous woman on the loose, he thought with an edge of self-contempt.

They heard footsteps and suddenly two guests appeared at the door. "Abby?" one said, then stopped abruptly when she saw Quincy. "Never mind. Talk to you later."

"That's okay," she said, but they were already on their way back to the house. Abby stepped outside, blinking in the bright sunshine. She turned to Quincy, who was looking off into the distance.

"Thanks again for the lesson. Next time . . ."

"You'll do it yourself."

"Yes, I hope so." She glanced at her watch and hurried along the path. Dinner would be late. She could blame it on the power failure. She could blame it on the generator, or she could blame it on herself for losing track of time while standing in the shed with a tall cowboy who was definitely, inexplicably, afraid of spiders. Quincy McLoud afraid of something. It was incredible, unimaginable. A smile quirked the corners of her mouth. It made him seem almost human.

Chapter Three

Quincy didn't see Abby until dinner and then he didn't see much of her since she had a huge white apron wrapped around her that covered her from neck to knees. She hurried in and out of the kitchen while he ate eggplant that was covered with red sauce and topped with cheese. Quincy wanted to ask about the main course, until he realized that was it. He carried a plate over to Pop, along with a bowl of green salad. The old man was leaning back in a recliner chair with his stocking-clad feet propped up in front of the television set when he saw Quincy come through the doorway. He switched it off immediately, leaning forward, but Quincy waved him back.

"Stay there. I'll get you something to eat on." He picked up a piece of shelving in the corner and laid it across Pop's lap. Then he set the salad and main dish in front of him. "I hope you're not very hungry," Quincy said, taking the chair across from him. "That's all there is."

Pop nodded. "Told ya things have changed. Me, I've got used to her cooking this past year. Even before the guests came she cooked this way. Plenty of vegetables, light on the meat."

"Did you hear what happened today?" Quincy asked, watching Pop attack his eggplant with gusto.

"You mean, the power pole coming down? Yeah, I heard, but ya know, you gotta give 'em credit for trying."

"For trying what, to smash the truck?"

"I mean they're tryin' to have a good time and this here's a working ranch."

"That's the problem. Those guests don't belong here and neither does she."

Pop put his fork down and frowned at Quincy. "You two getting on okay?"

"More or less."

Pop nodded. "I was thinkin' ya ought to move into Cookie's old room under the back stairs."

"In the ranch house?"

"Sure, why not? Ya got yer own entrance that way, and a bathroom. And yer near the kitchen in case ya get hungry at night. There's always something left over."

"More eggplant. Just what I wanted. Besides, I doubt Abby would like having me in the house."

"That's where yer wrong. I asked her about it when she come over this afternoon. She said it was okay by her. She seen there's not enough room for you here, long as you're stayin'."

Quincy ran his hand through his hair. He began to wonder if it was worth staying. Could he stand the humiliation of sleeping in the cook's quarters when by rights he should be upstairs in the master bedroom? Maybe he didn't have the patience to wait it out, after all. "Did she say I was staying?" he asked.

"Didn't say you wasn't."

"I'll wait till she mentions it. In the meantime I've got my sleeping bag. Your floor's not bad." That way he could keep his options open. The option to go, the option to stay.

When Quincy took the empty dishes back to the kitchen, the women had adjourned to the meeting room again, and this time he steered clear of the activities of cows. He especially didn't want her to see *him*, to clue in to the fact he was critical of what she was doing. Besides, he couldn't stand to watch her draw her imaginary circle around an imaginary cow. As if that helped when you were in a corral with a few hundred *real* cows.

Instead he took a look at the cook's old room, which adjoined the kitchen. It was dusty, but there wasn't a spider in sight and it *was* roomy. With windows on two sides, even if it wasn't as roomy as the bedroom upstairs with its walk-in closets and master bath. He thought of Abby up there and he wondered that she'd even want him under the same roof. He couldn't figure her out. One minute she was stiff and prickly, the next she'd laughed and teased him like they were old friends.

Her falling against him happened so fast he hadn't had time to react. If he had, what would he have done? Crushed her to him to feel her breasts pressed against his chest, to feel her thighs against his? Not a chance. He had more sense than that. He didn't used to have any when it came to women. Now he had plenty. He even had a sixth sense that warned him to back off. Very useful in situations like this.

He remembered when he thought marriage was forever. If you couldn't trust your wife, who could you trust? No one. He closed the door to the cook's quarters and walked around the house, his thoughts still on his new employer. The word "boss" stuck in his throat.

On the plus side, she wasn't afraid of spiders and she could ride. She had beautiful hair, more blond than brown in the sunlight, and under lamplight in the kitchen, it shone like pure gold. Despite his good intentions, he had a strong urge to just walk by the bunkhouse to see if they were still there. To see what she'd been wearing under that apron tonight.

But he forced himself to keep walking, around the pigpen, behind the chicken coop and around the barn again until he finally saw the lights go on in the big house. He ended up back at Pop's feeling jumpy and too keyed up to get into his sleeping bag and lie on the floor.

Pop was having trouble sleeping himself. He wouldn't say so, but Quincy knew his joints were aching by the way he tossed and turned.

"Have you taken anything?" Quincy asked, standing at the edge of Pop's narrow bunk.

Pop nodded. "But I wished I'd kept that hot water bottle Abby loaned me. She told me to, but I give it back."

"I'll get it for you."

Pop shook his head. "Too late. She'd be asleep by now."

"No, I just saw her lights go on. They must have had a long meeting."

Pop's thin lips twisted in pain. "Okay, if it's not too much trouble."

Quincy made his way down the dirt path in the dark, his eyes on the light in the upstairs window of the master bedroom that overlooked the fields and the hills beyond. His room. Her room now. Why not? She'd paid for it, she was entitled to enjoy it along with the extra-long, claw-foot porcelain tub a six-foot-three-inch man could submerge in up to his neck, or a tall woman for that matter. Or both of them at the same time. Not that he'd ever tried it. His ex-wife had been the brisk-shower-in-the-morning type. What type was Abby?

As he watched he saw the outline of her body against the curtains and he drew in a sharp breath. Her profile sent his thoughts straight through the sky, those firm upturned breasts, slim hips and long legs— He stumbled over a root and caught himself before he fell and rolled in the dirt.

Get a grip, he told himself. This woman is your boss and women are not to be trusted. If she knew you were thinking of her as a sex object, she'd send you packing. She may, anyway. But in the meantime he had a job to do. He banged on the front door. No answer. He opened it and walked up the front stairs, his boots hitting the wide varnished steps with loud, sharp cracks. He didn't want to sneak up on her or startle her, but in a medical emergency you couldn't stand on ceremony. At the top of the stairs he called her name. No answer.

He turned left and went to the end of the hall. When he knocked on the bedroom door, it took a long time before she finally answered. She appeared at the door wearing only a huge terry-cloth robe cinched at the waist. Skin moist and dewy, her hair escaped in tendrils from a huge white towel wrapped around her head. Her eyes widened in surprise, and he thought his knees might give way just imagining her in that bathtub.

"What's wrong?" she asked.

"It's Pop. He's not doing too well. He wonders if he could borrow your hot water bottle again."

"Of course. I'll get it."

When she disappeared into the bathroom he looked around the room. There was a four-poster bed where their double bed had been. It was covered with a soft comforter and ruffled pillows, dozens of them, and he wondered what she wore to bed. A long, lacy gown that you could see through? A short, satin whatchamacallit with thin straps over the shoulders? Nothing at all? His mouth was so dry he caught himself panting. Better focus on something else, anything else. She'd be back in a minute, back from the bathroom where he'd interrupted her bath. Now he had to fight off the image of all five foot ten inches of her stretched out in his tub, wearing nothing at all.

Before he knew it, she was back with a large red hot water bottle and had brushed past him on her way out the door. "I'll heat the water on the stove for you. Is it his knees?" she asked over her shoulder.

He followed closely behind her, the smell of garden flowers in her wake, filling the air, clouding his senses. "Knees? No, it's his neck and shoulders."

"I shouldn't have let him help me. But he insisted. He's such a hard worker, and so stubborn."

He followed her to the kitchen, remembering that Pop had described Abby as stubborn, too. And yet there was respect and admiration on both sides. Abby filled a teakettle and put it on the front burner. She leaned back against the tiled countertop and folded her arms across her waist.

"Yes, he is," Quincy said, wondering if she had anything on under that robe. Or was there just soft terry cloth against softer skin? He had an irrepressible urge to grasp the lapels of the robe and narrow the gap between them. Either that or untie the sash and find out once and for all what was underneath. With a great effort, he swallowed and focused on a copper pot hanging from a rack. "He never would have admitted anything was wrong," he continued. "He likes to talk, but not about himself."

Abby studied the man who was leaning against the chopping block counter surveying her with an unfathomable look. He was as lithe and well-muscled as a racehorse built for speed and power. The kind of man who was out to win the race, to get what he wanted. But what did he want? She knew he didn't like working for her and she suspected he didn't want to work for anybody. Then why was he here? Despite the warmth of the kitchen, she gave a little shiver of apprehension.

"He likes to talk about you, too," she commented.

He straightened and met her gaze. "Me?" he asked warily. She'd caught him off guard.

She nodded. "When I was over there this afternoon, he told me you were decorated in the war."

"It wasn't much of a war and it wasn't much of a decoration."

"What was it like, or would you rather not talk about it?" she asked. She had to admit it, she was curious. It also didn't surprise her to hear he was a hero at all.

"The Gulf War? It was a giant fiasco for me. When I joined the reserves I thought I'd never be called up. No one did. The cold war was over. I did my one weekend a month and two weeks in the summer. It was a way of making some extra money and serving my country at the same time. But one day I was feeding cattle in three-foot drifts of snow, the next day after that I was sleeping in a tent in the middle of the desert in ninety-degree heat. I was in shock for weeks. When I came out of it there were missiles going off overhead. It was my crew that evacuated a hospital in Riyadh. That's how I got the medal."

He braced his hands on the edge of the chopping block and hoisted himself on top of it. "I was worried about what was happening back home. I never heard from my wife. I didn't know how the stock was doing. I'd never been away that long, and my ex-wife was the restless type. I didn't realize how restless." His forehead creased and his voice dropped.

Abby tried to picture him in a uniform with short-cropped hair, but she couldn't. He was born to be a cowboy, with hair brushing the back of his collar, wearing tight denims. She tried to picture him married, but she couldn't do that, either. He was too independent.

"And before I knew it," he continued, "it was over. The war, the marriage, everything."

"What happened, where'd you go?" she asked, two faint lines etched between her eyebrows.

"Utah, Arizona..." He didn't wait for the next question: why come back to Kansas? "I missed the tall grass and hills," he said. "Nobody understands that." He studied his boots, suddenly uncomfortable with the turn the conversation had taken.

"I do," she said impulsively.

He looked up and met her gaze and something passed between them. Something more than understanding, but not sympathy. Something that defied definition, that made the blood rush to her head and her heart pound erratically. Then the whistle blew and the teakettle filled the air with steam.

He jumped down off the wooden block and held the rubber flaps open while she filled the bottle with boiling water. He screwed the cap on, thanked her and went out the back door.

Abby walked slowly back up the stairs in the dark. In just a few minutes, she'd learned more about Quincy McLoud than she needed to know. *More* than she wanted to know. Why should she feel sorry for him because his wife walked out on him? He didn't feel sorry for her. And she was the one who was struggling to make this ranch a success, risking everything she had.

Tomorrow she'd get away from here and from him. She had to drive into town anyway. She opened her bedroom window and felt a cool wind rush in. For some reason it made her think of Quincy, who had breezed onto her ranch, and her life, without a single by-your-leave. She slammed it shut. Maybe Pop was right. There was a change in the weather coming.

The next day the atmosphere was charged with electricity. It was one of those late spring days when the cold winds from the Rockies collided with the hot humid air from the south. The atmosphere seemed to invigorate everyone. The women burst out of the bunkhouse for a hearty breakfast and set out determinedly to complete the inoculations.

Abby was a little worried about them doing it on their own, but it was better than doing it with Quincy's help, where they'd ooh and aah and he'd do all the work. But she didn't have much time to worry, she had to get an early start for town.

Her truck started up fine, but when she put her foot on the brake pedal, it went clear to the floor. She got out and went around to the back of the truck, bending over to observe the rear axle. There on the ground was a pool of greenish brake fluid. She closed her eyes and clamped her teeth shut. Why now? Why her? She heard footsteps as she was kneeling there in the dirt, running her hand over the broken brake line.

"What's wrong?"

She looked up at Quincy, biting back a frustrated oath. "The brake line's broken. I can't drive it."

"They must have backed over something sharp yesterday and torn it. It can be fixed."

"Now?"

"No, not now. I'll get you a new part in town. I'm going in, anyway, to get some more baling wire."

She stared at him. Of course he was free to come and go as he liked. She didn't know why she was surprised to hear he was going.

"Can I have a ride?" she asked.

"Well…" He'd been looking forward to going, but on his own. If he saw someone he knew, which was more than likely, they could blow his cover. And the thought of sitting in a car with her so close wasn't a great idea, either. But how could he refuse? What could he say? "Okay," he said reluctantly.

After checking to make sure the women would be fine, she met him in fifteen minutes at his truck behind the barn. She was pleased to see her guests hard at work, rebuilding their confidence. Now there was the matter of her own equilibrium. How to hang on to it during a long drive with Quincy.

For the first half hour it wasn't so bad. They chose a safe subject: the weather. He recalled Kansas ice storms in March with a windchill of minus ten, and tornadoes in June where rooftops were blown into the next county and trucks were picked up and tossed into ditches. She listened wide-eyed, knowing she couldn't top those stories.

"I'm from St. Louis. I know something about weather."

"Do you know about thunderstorms that can send a barn floating down the road like a barge?"

"No," she admitted. "But I know about snow up to the bedroom window and icicles hanging from the eaves, and ninety-degree heat with matching humidity in the summer."

"Is that where you learned to ride, in St. Louis?"

"No, I spent a summer at a ranch in Wyoming, a wonderful summer. That's where I learned to ride. I had lessons in everything else back home though, from ballet to sailing. What about you?"

"Never had lessons of any kind. Especially not ballet. Everything I know I learned by doing."

"I'd say you've learned quite a lot."

"I haven't learned anything about women, except to keep my distance."

"You picked the wrong job, then, working for me."

"Work is one thing," he said with a sidelong glance, "marriage is something else. But you already know that. What happened, did you marry the wrong person?"

She gave him a quick glance. He was looking at the road, just making conversation. She wasn't sure how the conversation had taken this personal turn, but she didn't know how to redirect it, either.

"*I* didn't marry the wrong person," she said, "*He* did. He was looking for a corporate wife. I didn't know what I wanted to be. But I found out what I *didn't* want to be."

"What's so bad about being a corporate wife? Going to parties and talking business?"

She leaned her head back against the seat, visions of herself in high heels, pearls and little black dresses flashing through her mind. "You have no idea."

"It must have been easier than running a bunch of ornery cattle through their paces," he persisted.

"You'd be surprised," she said, turning her head toward him. "Have you ever had forty for dinner, remembering who's supposed to sit next to whom, a couple of times a week, week after week? Talk about herd animals. I could have used a little cow psychology then. I thought I was doing all right, actually, but he didn't."

"And so you got a divorce."

"Yes, a quickie in Reno. I waited out the six weeks at a guest ranch. That was the best part of it." The worst part she didn't want to talk about, the pain of regret, the pain of failure. She'd failed at dinner parties, and she'd failed to get pregnant so she could produce an heir to the law office. Now she had her own life, her own ranch, and this time she was going to succeed. She stared out the side window without seeing the horses behind white fences or the power poles rushing by. She didn't know why she was confiding in this man. It certainly wasn't to get his sympathy. He didn't strike her as the sympathetic type.

"Was it a real working ranch?" he asked.

"The Lazy Susan? Yes, it was."

"Is that a person or the ranch?"

Funny how she'd pegged him for the strong silent type. He hadn't stopped asking questions since she got into the truck, after he'd described the weather system over the middle states.

"Both," she answered. "Lazy Susan ran the ranch with an iron hand. She was anything but lazy, and I saw what I wanted to do, what I wanted to be."

"So you're modeling yourself after this Lazy Susan."

"Oh, I'll never be what she is, but at least she gave me some direction. And getting back on a horse was the first step in the right direction."

"Magic has a temper," he admitted, "you're right about that. But you're not a bad rider."

Surprised, she turned to look at him. That couldn't have been a sincere compliment, could it? If it was, she'd have to remember it, it might be the last.

Billboards along the highway advertised the local feed and fuel store, the bar and grill, and the Grassroots Museum, and soon they were slowly driving down Main Street.

"You can let me out anywhere," she said. "I've got things to do all over town."

He slowed and pulled over to the curb in front of the five-and-dime. "Why don't I meet you in front of the coffee shop at noon?" he asked.

She nodded and hopped down from the truck without a backward glance. He sat for a long time watching her go, moving down the street with an easy, unselfconscious grace. She was clearly unaware of the glances in her direction, of the heads that turned to watch her. She didn't know how good she looked with her blond hair blowing in the breeze, her long legs accentuated by her snug jeans and hand-tooled boots.

If he hadn't heard her story, just by seeing her walk down the street, he'd have sworn that she was born to this life. But then he'd thought that about Corinne, who was Kansas born and bred. And look what had happened to him. She'd cut out at the first opportunity. He had to admit it. Working the ranch was a hard, continuous task, and his being out with the reserves hadn't helped any. But, dammit, when had he ever claimed it would be easy? And didn't serving his country, hell, even making ends meet with the extra money they paid him, count for something?

He turned the truck toward the hardware store to pick up a new fence tightener and an ax, shutting his mind to the bitter part. It was his first time back in town since he'd left, a whole lifetime ago, and he was determined to enjoy it. He stuffed his hands into his back pockets and approached the store. He didn't need to worry about his welcome. The men sitting on the bench in front of the store stood and shook his hand.

"If it ain't the war hero."

"He come back in one piece at least."

"Far as we can see."

Quincy grinned and they slapped him on the back.

"Heard you was back."

"How'd you hear that? It's only been a few days," Quincy said.

Charlie Olson snapped his red suspenders. "News travels fast. What about that gal who bought your land? You hanging around to get better acquainted?" he asked with a wink.

"No way," Quincy said. "I'm just passing through. Giving her a hand while Pop's laid up."

"Give her more than that while you're at it," Charlie suggested. "I reckon it gets kinda lonely out there for a single woman."

Quincy froze and clenched his fists. He didn't want the town buzzing with gossip about him and Abby. If Charlie wasn't twenty years older and fifty pounds heavier than himself, he might have made that perfectly clear, but there was no sense stirring up trouble no matter what people were saying.

"Good to see you," he said instead, and walked into the store, leaving behind several subdued faces and an awkward silence. When he came out they'd disbursed and he went to the car parts store where he was again greeted warmly before they got down to what was on everybody's minds.

"About that woman who bought your place..."

"Yeah, what about her?" he asked.

"Is it true she's got a whole passel of women on the place this week? When's she gonna give us a break and bring 'em into town?"

He shook his head. "She's keeping them busy doing chores."

"How's it feel to be back?" someone asked, knowing full well it must feel like hell to be a hired hand on your own place.

"Fine," he said. But it *wasn't* easy. Pretend it didn't hurt to have your land sold out from under you, to have your wife take off the minute your back was turned? Tell yourself it was worth coming back because it was still the most beautiful land in Kansas, maybe in the world? No, it wasn't easy. His smile grew grim.

"Bet you'd do anything to get the place back."

"Almost," he agreed absently, and then it happened. A plan formed in his mind. What if things continued to go wrong at the ranch and the guests all left and Abby couldn't make her payments to the bank? She'd *have* to sell, wouldn't she? And who would she sell to, somebody off the street, or the man who was working at her side, who had her trust and her confidence. Him. And if things didn't go wrong fast enough, he might be able to speed them up.... His conscience tweaked, but he ruthlessly quieted it. He would just be helping her realize she couldn't handle things sooner rather than later, that was all. It was for her own good. It was worth a try.

Meanwhile Abby was at the power company, which was housed in a brick building just off Main Street, explaining the problem she had and insisting that they come out right away and fix it. They said next Monday. She said Friday. They said they'd try. She said it was urgent.

"I hear Quincy McLoud is in town," the secretary said as she typed up the work order.

Abby's eyes widened in surprise. If she lived here a hundred years she'd never understand how news traveled so fast.

"Too bad about his wife dumping him," the woman remarked, looking up at Abby over the forms. "Especially when he was off fighting for his country."

Abby avoided answering by pretending interest in a brochure that explained how to save energy, but she couldn't avoid the next questions.

"Good-looking guy, don't you think?"

She swallowed hard. Of course he was a good-looking guy. But she didn't want her opinion broadcast all over town. What was the woman doing, anyway, taking a survey? "I didn't notice," she said primly. But she'd noticed. How could anybody not notice those shoulders, the rare smile that transformed his rugged features, and those gray eyes the color of smoke?

"He won't stay around here long," the woman said, handing Abby a copy of the work order, "do you think?"

"I suppose not," Abby said, grabbing the paper and leaving the office as fast as she could. He probably wouldn't stay around long at all. He'd probably take off whenever it suited him. Well, that was fine with her. She'd gotten along before he came and she'd get along after he left. She really didn't know why he was there at all, working for nothing for her.

She walked quickly down the street toward the coffee shop. It was almost noon and she felt light-headed. Maybe because she'd forgotten to eat breakfast.

Quincy was pacing back and forth on the sidewalk waiting for her. He opened the door to the coffee shop and held it for her. "Ready for some lunch?" he asked.

She hesitated. Not only did she not have money to eat in a restaurant, she didn't want to prolong her day alone with

Quincy. The less time for embarrassing questions about her past, the better.

"I don't know about you, but I didn't have breakfast," he told her as he guided her through the doorway, his hand resting lightly on her hip. "This is it," he said. "This is where everyone who is anyone eats." He stopped suddenly and looked around the familiar crowded diner. The place was packed with faces of people he knew, people who could give him away with just a word. He pulled his hat down over his forehead and, using Abby as a shield, moved with great haste toward the last booth in the far corner.

He slid onto the vinyl cushion with his back to the rest of the restaurant. Why couldn't he have just ignored his hunger pangs and driven straight home? She wanted to, but he'd had to have lunch first. He didn't seem to be thinking very straight these days. He picked up the large laminated menu and held it up in front of his face. After a few minutes he lowered the menu a fraction of an inch and looked at Abby. She was looking at him with a puzzled expression. He couldn't blame her. He didn't understand himself sometimes.

"What do you recommend?" she asked.

"I recommend we eat as fast as possible and head for home," he said.

"That's fine with me," she said, and he realized how strange he was acting—one minute determined to take her to lunch, the next trying to hustle her out of there. Making an effort to forget about the possibility of being unmasked right there and then, he took his hat off and put his menu face down on the table.

"The specials are good, but I see it's meat loaf today. Do you eat meat?"

"Of course, I do. But when I'm cooking for women I try to make the kind of thing they'll like—light, healthy food. I haven't heard any complaints, have you?"

"Nope," he admitted, and he looked up into the eyes of the waitress.

She took one look at Quincy and rocked back on her heels. "Well, I'll be switched . . . if it isn't—"

"Hello, Dorothy," Quincy cut in smoothly. "I'll have the meat loaf, and the lady wants . . ."

"The soup of the day and a salad," Abby said.

To Quincy's dismay Dorothy didn't write a word on the small pad she held in her hands, she just stared at him as if she'd seen a ghost. "I can't believe my eyes," she said, shaking her head. "I didn't think you'd ever be back in these parts, not after—"

"Had to come back if I ever wanted a good meal again. You wouldn't believe how they treat food in the U.S. Army. How come this is the only place in the world that knows how to make a decent meat loaf?"

"Now, Quincy . . ."

"It's true. And the apple pie. Bring us two pieces, would you?"

Dorothy nodded and started writing at last. All she had to do was say something about the ranch and he'd had it. He'd be back on his way, leaving behind one bewildered woman who would wonder why he'd kept the truth from her. If only Dorothy would just take their orders and disappear like a normal waitress, but instead she'd turned her attention to Abby and was staring at her with a puzzled frown. Didn't she know who she was? Was she going to stand there staring until she figured it out?

"Anything to drink?" Dorothy asked.

"I'll have coffee with my pie," Abby said.

Dorothy scribbled something with her pencil and turned to go, but before Quincy could heave a sigh of relief, she turned back to their table. "Say," she said to Abby, "aren't you . . . ?"

"The new owner of the Bar Z," Abby said quietly.

"Well I'll be danged," Dorothy said, looking from Quincy to Abby and back again. "I'll be gol-danged." Shaking her head, she finally disappeared behind the swinging doors into the kitchen.

Quincy looked at Abby. To his relief, she was smiling. "I get that all the time," she said. "People can't believe a woman can own and run a ranch."

"Wonder why?" Quincy asked, still worried that he wasn't out of danger yet.

"You know why," she explained, taking a sip of water. "People think ranching is men's work. Even you have doubts sometimes. Admit it."

"I try to keep an open mind," he said modestly.

"That's not to say I don't have moments when I'm afraid," she continued.

"Afraid of what?" he asked. But he didn't want to know. He didn't want to hear about her fears or feel any sympathy for her. She was standing between him and what was rightfully his. It was bad enough her hair was the color of sunflowers here in the Sunflower State. It was bad enough her eyes were the color of the Kansas sky. She still didn't belong here. He had no objection to her having a ranch as long as it wasn't his. But no, she'd had to fall in love with his ranch.

Did she really know what love was? He didn't. It had been a long time since he'd fallen in love and not that long since he'd fallen out of love.

She was twisting her fingers together before she spoke. "Afraid of not making it. Afraid the guests won't have a good time."

"Then why have guests? Why not run it as a cattle ranch, as it was meant to be run?"

"I thought of that. That's what Pop wanted to do. But I want city people to have the experience I had—that changed my life, that gave me the confidence I needed to start over. If I can help just one person..."

Dorothy came with Abby's soup, which put an end to the discussion, and Quincy was glad. He didn't want to hear her philosophy of life. He didn't want to hear how the ranch had turned her around. He was even gladder to see his meat loaf appear, next to a pile of mashed potatoes smothered in gravy. And this time Dorothy was too busy to talk. She just plunked the plates in front of them and hurried off.

Abby seemed to be enjoying her lunch, he thought, sliding a glance at her from across the table. Maybe she'd never eaten here before. She looked up and met his gaze.

"Did I tell you who's coming next week?"

"Coming, to the ranch? I don't believe you did."

"It's Single Parents' Week," she said with a smile.

"How did that happen?" he asked incredulously. "Have you forgotten that calving starts next week?"

"Of course not," she said. "I timed it that way. So the kids can play with the new calves."

"What kids?"

She leaned against the back of the booth and gave him an impatient look. "The children of the single parents. That's what it's all about."

"That's funny, I thought it was all about calving, about delivering as many healthy calves as possible. This is still a cattle ranch we're talking about, isn't it?"

"Of course. With one significant difference. It's a cattle ranch with guests. And calving could be one of the most exciting and emotional experiences of a lifetime. For anyone."

"Have you been through it?" he asked as calmly as he could, knowing she hadn't, knowing she didn't know what she was talking about.

She hesitated. "No, but I've heard a lot about it. I suppose you've done it a hundred times."

"More or less."

"And how would you describe it?" she challenged.

"As hard work. The hardest work you'll ever do, if you do it."

"Of course, I'll do it. It's practically the whole reason I bought the ranch. To watch the miracle of birth."

He shook his head in disgust. "Why didn't you buy a pregnant dog or cat? It would have been a lot cheaper."

"Of course, but you know what I mean. You must or you wouldn't be a cowboy."

"I know that calving is a twenty-four-hour-a-day job. And if the weather doesn't cooperate, it's a cold, wet, messy job. There are accidents, there are mishaps and there are mistakes. I'll need all the help I can get just to get through it."

"You'll have it. You'll have Curly and Rocky and you'll have the single parents and their kids."

"I thought they were coming to *watch* the miracle of birth."

"They're coming to work on a ranch. That means whatever work there is."

"Can you really see them getting up in the middle of the night to sit through a difficult breech delivery? It's not a pretty sight."

She frowned. "Maybe not. But I will. I don't want to miss a single moment."

"I'll remember that," he promised her.

Neither of them spoke while Dorothy cleared their plates and brought pie and coffee.

Then Quincy continued. "Have you ever thought of what you'd do if you had to choose between a guest ranch and a working ranch?"

"I know which one you'd choose. You think there's no place for guests on a cattle ranch, don't you? Well, that just makes me more determined to show you you're wrong."

She didn't have to tell him that. He could see the determination blazing in her eyes and it made him wonder about his tactics so far. What would it take to make her give in, give up and sell the place back to him? Whatever it was, it was best she took him for the wandering cowhand he pretended to be rather than the former owner trying to grab his ranch back. Now if he could just get out of town without someone identifying him, he could get back to work. Good thing Pop had warned Curly and Rocky, but he couldn't expect Pop to warn the whole town.

Fortunately they got out of the restaurant and out of town without any further incident. Quincy refrained from making any more derogatory comments about the combination of single parents and calving. He'd warned her, he'd told her it wouldn't work, and she couldn't blame him when it all fell apart.

The only time she spoke on the way home was after they'd driven a half hour or so in silence.

"I know how you feel about me," she said pensively.

Startled, Quincy glanced at her. "You do?"

"You haven't tried to keep your disapproval a secret, but I can accept that. And I appreciate your honesty. I can deal with disapproval, but not dishonesty." She stared straight ahead toward the hills in the distance. A glance at her profile told him nothing except she meant what she said. He didn't look forward to the day she found out he'd been lying to her from the moment they'd met.

Chapter Four

At the end of Women's Week Abby scanned the faces as the guests said goodbye in front of the ranch house. She was looking for something she didn't find. A certain something, a look in the eyes that told her she'd changed someone's life, the way hers had been changed by the Lazy Susan. She saw regret at leaving, she saw gratitude, but she didn't see any transformations.

On the other hand, she'd gotten through the week without any more major mishaps. The power was back, the telephone, too. Her truck had been repaired, thanks to Quincy. And, thanks to Quincy, the cattle had all been inoculated. Not that he'd bragged about anything he'd done. She'd found out about these things indirectly. In fact they had hardly exchanged a word during the rest of the week, but she couldn't deny that everything moved more smoothly now that he was there.

He was only a shadowy presence on the periphery of her vision. A long, tall, lean shadow at the kitchen table with Pop and the boys in the morning and in the evening. Aside from that she only knew he was there by the incredible amount of work he got done. She began to feel guilty about not paying him.

After the last guest had left she made lunch and when Quincy came into the kitchen, she put a large wooden bowl on the table in the breakfast nook and sat down across from him. Surprised, he looked up at her.

"I thought since the guests are gone, I'd join you all for lunch," she explained.

"Pop took off a little while ago. And the boys took sandwiches out to the pasture with them." He paused. "Do you want to change your mind?"

"About sitting here? No, you're the one I want to talk to." She nodded at the salad bowl. "Help yourself."

He peered into the bowl. "Spinach? You didn't have to go to all that trouble for me," he said, heaping a mound of bright green leaves with fresh mushrooms, chopped egg and a bit of bacon onto his plate. Then he tilted his head back and looked at her. "What did you want to talk to me about?"

"I wanted to thank you for all you've done this week. It just doesn't seem right, my not paying you when you work harder than anybody."

"I thought you couldn't afford to pay me."

"Is there something else you want, something I could do for you?"

He stared at her, lengthening and deepening the silence between them while he pondered the question until she wished she'd never asked. Things were going so well, she'd almost forgotten how his presence could affect her, especially when they were alone together, here in this cozy nook, just the two of them across the table from each other. The only sound was the ticking of the clock on the wall and her words hung in the air. If there was something he wanted, maybe she didn't want to know what it was.

"I'm here because I want to be," he said at last, "because I like this place."

She nodded. "Almost as much as I do."

"Maybe more."

"Still, it doesn't seem fair..." she trailed off. She didn't know what to say, what to suggest. All she could do was stare at him, at his sun-bronzed high cheekbones, his strong jaw and molded mouth, and wonder what he was thinking. She was tired. The guests had taken a lot out of her and she was relieved to have a moment to breathe. It was so quiet in the house. All over the ranch there was a silence that permeated the atmosphere. And every word either one of them said seemed loaded with meaning.

Unexpectedly he reached out and covered her hand with his. "Don't worry about it," he said.

She felt the roughness of his palm and her hand shook under his. The grandfather clock in the parlor chimed and shook her out of her reverie. She slid her hand out from under his and took a large bite of spinach salad. She really shouldn't eat in the kitchen. It was too small, too intimate, and Quincy had an effect on her she couldn't deny and she couldn't handle. She should really avoid all unnecessary contact with him, which would be easy once the new group arrived. Tomorrow. She just had to avoid him until tomorrow. They ate their salad and then they went their separate ways, but she wondered if that was the end of the discussion.

Quincy went to check on the pregnant cows; Abby went to do the laundry and clean the bunkhouse for the new arrivals. She hung the sheets on the line to dry in the bright sunshine behind the house, enjoying the smell of the grass and the breeze that ruffled her hair. Soaking in the solitude that would last only one day, she planned activities with a clothespin clamped in her mouth: feeding chickens, collecting eggs, riding, hiking... and seeing calves being born, if the cows would cooperate.

After Quincy checked the last cow, he left the barn and came around the corner of the ranch house for dinner that evening, sniffing the air. He didn't know what to expect for dinner that night, but he knew he was hungry. Raw spinach might be enough for women who were watching their weight, but it didn't really last him through the day.

At least, whatever they were having, he wouldn't be alone with Abby. Pop was back and the boys would be in for dinner, too. Thank God. He couldn't take many more of those intimate meals with Abby. For one thing, it was awkward discussing what she owed him. It made him feel guilty. What would she have done if he'd asked for a salary? He knew she couldn't give him one, so what could she have had in mind when she'd asked him what he'd wanted? She couldn't have any idea of what he really wanted, and he hoped she wouldn't until the place fell apart.

He could see it happening soon. Maybe even next week, when she realized that kids and calves didn't mix. A smile of anticipation began forming on his face, only to be replaced by a frown at his next thought. She was a dreamer. He could see it in her blue eyes and hear it in her voice. And dreamers didn't belong on cattle ranches. So why did the thought disturb him so? Impatient with himself, he walked faster. Abby's making a go of the ranch was a foregone conclusion in the negative; there was no reason to feel guilty about anything. In fact, he would be doing her a service by hanging around and being the one to offer to buy her out once she realized her mistake.

Inordinately pleased with his reasoning, he again turned his thoughts to dinner. He was hungry. There was no one in the kitchen when he walked in, just the sound of loud voices and laughter from the dining room. He peered through the window in the door and saw everyone sitting around the table: Curly, Rocky, Pop and Abby. He opened the door and let it swing shut. They all looked up.

"Where've ya been?" Pop asked, smiling his toothy grin. "We thought ya got lost. Even the boys made it back tonight. Don'tcha know there's meat loaf for dinner?"

He nodded abruptly. He knew. He'd smelled it the moment he'd stepped into the kitchen. He also knew that Abby had left her apron in the kitchen and was wearing a ribbed, long-sleeved shirt with soft, clean, wheat-colored jeans. And that they'd saved a place for him across from his boss where he'd have to eat her meat loaf and plan to take her ranch away from her at the same time. Guilt stabbed at him, and he moved restlessly. Dammit, he'd been through this already. He wasn't supposed to feel guilty about taking back something that was his.

All through dinner the others laughed and talked and he ate without saying anything. If they noticed his silence, it didn't bother them. But it bothered him. It bothered him so much he had a hard time meeting Abby's gaze. The only time he looked at her was when she wasn't looking at him.

Curly regaled the others with some local gossip about the church organist and the school principal and Quincy envied their carefree banter. But he couldn't afford to be carefree, he reminded himself grimly. He had his future to think of. So he ate his meat loaf and left them at the table, drinking coffee, still talking, still laughing.

He made the rounds of the pregnant cows in the barn before heading for his sleeping bag on Pop's floor. None of the cows were due quite yet, but he'd noticed one fidgety cow in particular who'd stopped eating that morning. It could mean she was ready. When he found her, he knew he'd been right. She was moaning softly and was lying on her side. He slid his hand along her udder and frowned. It felt uncomfortably swollen and rigid. Turning the overhead lights on, he quickly but gently led her into a clean box stall. Then he stepped outside and looked up at the ranch house. The house was dark and the night air cool and still. The thought to call the cow's owner crossed his mind, but then, he'd pulled many a calf alone and he saw no reason to disturb Pop or Abby.

On the other hand, how could he *not* disturb her when the miracle of birth was one of the main reasons she'd bought the ranch? Hesitating briefly, he made up his mind swiftly, telling himself he'd changed his mind only because when she saw the messy birth process it would help *him* out. She might realize that ranching wasn't as romantic as she'd thought, it was just part of life on a ranch. He walked quickly to the house, knocked on the front door, though he knew she couldn't hear him, and then entered, going up the front staircase. A small part of him betrayed him, hoping she'd say she was too tired to sit around waiting for a calf to be born, but he doubted that would be the case.

He knocked softly on her bedroom door and it was only a few seconds before she opened it. It was so dark in the room he was only aware of a long, loose nightgown, a cloud of blond hair and the smell of those flowers, her own special fragrance.

"Quincy?" she asked breathlessly.

"We've got a cow that may be ready," he said brusquely. "I thought you'd want to know."

"Oh, yes, of course," she said, smiling. "I'll get dressed."

He turned on his heel, his stomach tightening at the sight of her warm smile. "I'll wait downstairs."

He'd barely hit the last step when she joined him, wearing a T-shirt and jeans and carrying her shoes. He watched as she sat on the floor and tied the laces.

"How much time have we got?" she whispered.

He shrugged in the darkness, and then they hurried out the front door. "It could be hours or it could be minutes," he said, taking long strides toward the barn. He already regretted the impulse that had taken him into the ranch house.

It turned out to be hours. The cow strained, but no water bag broke. They sat, they stood, they walked back and forth, but they didn't talk. There wasn't much to say. At one point Abby sat on a bale of hay in the corner of the barn and leaned her head back against the wall and closed her eyes. Only then did he allow his gaze to travel her way. Only then did he see that her T-shirt was pulled tight across her full breasts, revealing their lush fullness and perfect shape. He swallowed hard. So she hadn't had time to put on a bra. Did that mean he had to stare at her as if he'd never seen a woman in a T-shirt before?

Her eyes suddenly flew open, as if she knew he was undressing her with his eyes, and she sat upright. He jerked his gaze away just in time and went down on his knees to check on the cow.

"What's happening?" she asked, getting to her feet and crouching down next to him.

Quincy massaged the cow's udder with careful fingers. Her distress had increased considerably. "It's coming out backward," he said tensely.

Her eyes widened with fear. "Is that bad?"

"It could be, but I've pulled calves out backward before. Something's wrong beside that, though. She doesn't seem to have the energy to push anymore."

"Should I call the vet?"

He shook his head. "Nothing he can do, it's just— Oh, here we go."

The back legs were inching their way out the birth canal, and with Quincy's help, the rest of the calf came. Abby swallowed nervously. There *was* something very wrong. There was no crying, no movement. Abby's shoulder pressed against his, and her hip rubbed against Quincy's as she watched him pull the calf entirely from its mother.

"What is it? What's wrong?" Abby asked in an anguished voice.

"He's dead, Abby. I'm sorry," Quincy told her flatly.

She rocked back on her heels and her eyes filled with tears. "But why?"

He wrapped the stillborn calf in a burlap sack, and Abby leaned back against a pile of hay. "He's too small, only about half normal weight, I'd guess, and then it was a breech delivery, never easy."

"Oh, no...I thought...you said..." Tears rushed to her eyes. She knew it was pointless to cry. This was all a part of ranching, but the sight of the very still bundle in the corner tugged at her heartstrings, and she couldn't help it. Silently, she cried as she grasped what had happened. Quincy cleaned up with the bucket of water he'd brought earlier and set aside. Then he pulled Abby up from where she sat on the ground and caught her tears with the pads of his thumbs.

Something inside him had gone still at the sight of Abby's tears. He hated to lose a calf, but he hated to see her cry even more. It made him feel sick inside. Gently, he turned her face to his. "Abby, I said I'd done it before. It usually turns out okay, but this time it didn't."

Her face was red and blotchy, her forehead covered with delicate etched lines, but she had never been more beautiful to him. "Wasn't there something we could have done?" she asked. "Maybe if we'd pulled it out right away instead of waiting..."

"Abby," he said, running his hands down her arms, "we can't play 'if only.' If only we'd called the vet, if only we'd monitored her better... The truth is there probably wasn't anything we could have done for her." His eyes turned dark and his hands tightened on her arms. "I'm sorry, I shouldn't have called you."

She stiffened and pulled away. "Yes, you should. It's my cow and my calf and I want to be a part of this ranch, of everything that happens on it. The good and the bad, only I...I..."

Oh, God, she was going to cry again. "I know," he interrupted quickly, "how you want to be a part of it, but it isn't always going to be easy. You'll get your chance to witness the miracle of birth, I promise. But it won't make up for this one, because every life is important, and we don't want to lose a single one."

She looked at him with bleary, red-rimmed eyes and he could almost see her pull herself up and straighten her shoulders. He wanted to take her in his arms, to feel her heartbeat against his, to tell her everything was going to be all right, but knew he couldn't. Nobody could promise her that. She had to learn that life and death were a very real part of a ranch. So why was *he* the one hurting for her?

She blew her nose and pressed her lips tightly together and that was when he knew she was going to be all right. He still wanted to hold her to him and feel the warmth of her body through her shirt, but he knew better. He couldn't trust himself to just offer comfort. Right now she needed him and he couldn't take advantage of that need. He took a step backward.

"I'll take care of everything. You go back to bed," he said.

She hesitated, then sighed. "Okay...and, Quincy? Thanks for coming to get me and thanks for doing everything you could." Her eyes glittered with unshed tears but she managed a half smile and he nodded before he turned to take care of the cow who'd lost her baby. There was work yet to be done. Dwelling on the warm feeling her words and soft, dewy eyes had created in his insides was *not* on the agenda.

"Good night," he said without looking up. He heard her footsteps echo through the barn, but he didn't raise his head until he was sure she was gone. She had guts, that woman, and she was a fast learner. One of these days she'd be delivering calves all by herself. Which was not what he wanted, he reminded himself. The thought shouldn't make him proud. Then she could replace *him* instead of him replacing *her*. If he weren't so tired, he might be worried.

When he dragged himself out of his sleeping bag the next morning, Pop was gone and he was alone in the small, one-room shed. He knew it was late, but his eyes stung and his mouth was as dry as a cotton willow. He'd slept only a few hours, and it hadn't been an easy sleep. As much as he'd tried not to, he was troubled by the death of the calf and its effect on Abby.

He pulled clean jeans over his sore, aching joints and put on a work shirt before he walked across the way to the house. Pop and Curly and Rocky were sitting at the breakfast table eating cold cereal and milk. Where was Abby? Where was the warmth from the oven, the smell of hot muffins or French toast? Where was her smile, her own brand of sunshine? He soon found out.

"She's out clearing a hiking trail for the kids coming today. Said she had no time for breakfast. Said she hoped we didn't mind," Pop said. The glum looks on their faces told Quincy they did mind, and so did he. What disturbed him was the gut-deep certainty his complaint with the situation wasn't solely on account of having to eat a cold breakfast. He poured some cereal and then milk into his bowl, not liking the beginning to the day already.

"Heard what happened last night," Rocky said.

"It happens," Quincy said briefly, stirring the cereal with his spoon.

"You could have called one of us," Curly said.

"Or me," Pop chimed in, "instead of Abby."

"She wanted to come," Quincy said. "It wasn't my idea. And I didn't need any help. There wasn't anything anyone could have done. It was breech and it was stillborn— Why? What did Abby say?"

"Not much," Pop said, looking unhappy. Rocky frowned and Curly stared at Quincy. Quincy had the uncomfortable feeling that they thought he'd done wrong by calling Abby. Of course if he'd known what was going to happen he wouldn't have, but as he'd said, she'd *wanted* to come.

After breakfast Pop went to the pasture, while Curly and Quincy walked to the barn together.

"No doubt about it," Curly said, "we're going to have some calves today."

Quincy nodded. There were going to be some miracles and soon, and that ought to make Abby happy. The thought made him smile, which made him frown. What did he care if she was happy? Nonetheless, that afternoon when he heard that Pop had delivered a pair of twin heifers, he headed straight for him. The older man was just washing up when Quincy found him.

"Does Abby know?" Quincy asked the old man.

He shook his head. "I looked around for her, but couldn't find her. I guess she's still busy getting ready for the group. This mornin' she sure looked anxious. 'Bout as anxious as you, wonderin' how we're going to make it without the usual crew."

"Yeah," Quincy agreed. "If it were up to me I'd hire some more help. But what can I do when she can't afford it? Offer to pay for them myself?"

Pop slanted him a concerned look. "It's hard on you bein' in charge and yet not bein' in charge. How long ya gonna keep it up?"

Quincy shrugged casually. "Depends."

"We all know you wasn't meant to be nobody's cowhand. You deserve to get yer place back. But danged if I can see how yer gonna do it. Ya got one determined little lady to deal with here. Yep, one anxious, determined little lady."

Quincy nodded and went back to work. There was no time to worry about how to get the place back today. There was too much work to do.

At lunchtime, the men staggered into the kitchen. Smelling food cooking, Quincy breathed a sigh of relief. At least Abby was back. She was frying up corned beef hash for them topped with fresh poached eggs.

But she didn't sit down and eat, and never spoke directly to Quincy. Her eyes still looked red around the edges and he never saw her smile. Not once.

"Pop delivered a pair of heifers this morning," he said, going to the stove to refill his plate. She didn't turn to face him, but out of the corner of his eye he noticed she held her spatula tightly in her hand.

"How are they?" she asked brightly.

"Fine," Pop answered. "I'll bring 'em over to the lot next to the house when yer guests get here. They might like to pet them."

"Don't you want to see them?" Quincy asked her.

"Maybe later. I'm pretty busy right now," she said.

"Sorry we can't help you more, but calving is our busiest time," he said, then could have kicked himself. Why was he apologizing? It *was* the busiest time on a ranch. He'd already told her that, and the sooner she learned it, the better for them all.

"Yes, I know, and I think it'll all work out. Remember, I want the guests to help you do whatever you're doing."

"Like shoveling manure?" Rocky asked, then doubled up with laughter.

Abby managed a faint smile.

Quincy went back to the table. It was going to be an interesting week, one in which they would all learn a lot. Hopefully Abby would learn that guests and calving didn't go together. Not that he wished her ill will, of course, just a hefty dose of reality, just enough to realize that she didn't belong on a ranch—not this one, anyway.

The week started peacefully enough. Pop put some of the new calves in the pen by the house where the children could play with them. When Quincy walked by, kids were sitting on the calves, hugging the calves and petting the calves. A half dozen parents were clustered at the fence taking pictures of their offspring cavorting with the animals. He heard Abby call to him from the other side of the fence and he approached cautiously.

"This is my right-hand man, Quincy McLoud," she told the guests. "I couldn't get along without him."

They shook his hand, they looked him over, they took his picture while he silently fumed. *Right-hand man?* He was *nobody's* right-hand man and it was galling to have city slickers gawk at him as if he were an exhibit in a museum.

"I didn't know there were any real cowboys left," one single mom murmured. "Can I have my picture taken with you?"

Quincy glared at Abby as she obligingly snapped the picture of him and the guest. Then the guest took several pictures of him and Abby. Abby could feel the tension in his body as his shoulder brushed against her arm.

"I feel like a damned idiot," he said out of the side of his mouth.

"You don't look like one," she said, with a smile for the camera. "You look like a real cowboy."

"So do Rocky and Curly."

"But they didn't happen to walk by."

"My mistake," he muttered as the guests arranged themselves around him for one more photo opportunity. Finally he tipped his hat and excused himself. Abby followed and caught up with him on his way to the feed lot.

"Would you have any time to help me bring out the horses for the guests?" she asked. "I know you're busy, but I just need your advice about which ones to choose. Then I'll leave you alone, I promise." She could see his face shutter down. "I know, the guests are my job and the calving yours, but sometimes they overlap—like today—when my guests want to play with your calves and want to ride your horses."

"And when your guests want to take my picture," he added.

"Was that so painful?" she asked curiously.

"Did I look like I was in pain?" he asked indignantly.

"Well..." The pictures were actually ones *she'd* like to have a copy of, the two of them surrounded by fresh new calves, so soft you just wanted to cuddle up with them. And tall, lean Quincy by her side, radiating masculinity and strength, eyes narrowed under the brim of his cowboy hat, mouth firm and smiling—

"Anyway," he said, bringing her back to reality with a thump. "They're not *your* guests and *my* cattle. They're *your* guests and *your* cattle. All yours," he added.

"Mine and the bank's," she said lightly. "And if I don't make it as both a guest rancher and a cattle rancher they'll be all the bank's."

Quincy gave her a look that disturbed her, as if he were calculating her chances for survival and found they weren't very good. After he left, she gave a little shiver of apprehension. It suddenly dawned on her that he was biased, prejudiced and dead set against her turning this place into a guest ranch and she'd be damned if she could understand why. But whatever his reason, she was going to prove him wrong.

Chapter Five

The day passed in a kaleidoscope of activities. After riding and kite flying and hiking, she served lasagna to the guests for dinner, then declared free time and collapsed on the wide front veranda of the old ranch house after they'd all eaten. Sinking down onto the porch swing, she finally caught her breath, going over the day's events in her mind. That afternoon, against his will, Quincy had brought out five of the gentlest horses and then hung around to give the kids some basic instructions in riding them.

She'd expected him to spend only a few minutes with the children, but the minutes had stretched to an hour and no matter what he'd said, she knew he'd been having a good time. While she was saddling a horse for a parent, she'd seen him holding the reins for a little girl and guiding her around the corral with something closely approaching infinite patience. More patience than he'd shown for anyone, except for the pregnant cow.

Her thoughts drifted. She wondered if Quincy had wanted children. Was he sorry he hadn't had any, or did horses and cows take their place in his life? She heard footsteps in the gravel and touched her toe to the floor to stop the swing.

"Abby?"

It was Quincy's deep voice. Squinting, she could just make out his tall, lean body standing in the driveway.

"Is anything wrong?" he asked.

"No, why?"

"I've never seen you not working, except when you were asleep."

"You've seen me asleep?" she asked.

"Last night on the hay."

"I wasn't sleeping, I was resting." She leaned forward. "I don't suppose any of those cows will calve tonight, will they?"

He rested one foot on the bottom step. "They might. I'll call you when it happens."

"Then we can call the kids. They'd love to see a calf being born."

"It's not always a pretty sight."

"I know that." It had taken her a day to get over the death of the calf and she still thought about it.

"I can't induce labor for their benefit."

"No, of course not. And there's plenty for them to do. Tomorrow they've got a hayride, a picnic, fishing in the creek. It's going to be fun."

"Fun? You look exhausted."

She wondered how he could tell in the twilight. She could hardly see his face at all, couldn't tell if he was exhausted or not. She only knew that the sound of his voice sent tremors through her body. Especially in the dark, especially when she was tired and her guard was down.

"Part of the experience here will be the memories it brings back . . . of that summer on the ranch. For most kids it's a dream, you know, going to a ranch. We get to make their dreams come true," she explained.

"We?"

"Yes, we. That's what you were doing when you showed that little girl how to ride today. Making her dreams come true. Giving her memories that will last forever. Don't pretend it was part of your job, either, Quincy McLoud. You told me it wasn't. But you like kids, don't you?"

"I don't know. I never had any." His reply was flat and quick, but she detected a strange note within it.

"Well, what about when you were one?"

"I can't remember that far back."

"Did you grow up on a ranch, or don't you remember that, either?"

Quincy paused and took a step up toward the porch. She could see his face now that her eyes were accustomed to the falling darkness, make out the faraway look in his gray eyes as he leaned against the railing.

"I grew up on a ranch," he said sharply, knowing he had to do something to stop the direction the conversation was taking. "And I remember the work, before school and after. It was always a struggle to make ends meet, just like it is now."

"Then you understand what I'm going through," she said softly.

"I don't understand *why* you're going through it," he replied quickly. Maybe this was his chance to get her to see what she was letting herself in for. But her next words sank his hopes like the *Titanic*.

"Yes, you do," she said quietly, digging her heels into the wide wooden planks of the porch. "You know how much it means to me and how much I love it. You say you don't understand, but what you mean is that you don't approve." She crossed her arms over her waist. She'd been feeling so good before he appeared out of the darkness. She was tired, yes, but at peace, and now he'd ruined it with his skepticism.

Without a word he took the next three porch steps in one long stride. He grasped the arms of the swing and leaned down, looking into her eyes, his face only inches from hers. "I don't disapprove of you, not personally. But I'm a cowboy, and cowboys deal with cows, not people. That's why

I'm here, to take care of the cows, so the ranch won't fall apart."

She looked into his smoky gray eyes and saw an intensity there that scared her. "Do you think it is falling apart?" she asked.

"I think it's a distinct possibility, unless we all work very hard."

"Work hard? I *am* working hard. How could any of us work any harder?"

He swung around and eased himself next to her on the swing, so smoothly that she was scarcely aware of it until he stretched his arm out behind her, his sleeve grazing her shoulders. "We can't, not with the staff we've got. So we just have to hope for the best, Abby."

She nodded, oddly pleased with his assessment. It would be an uphill battle, but maybe she'd imagined his opposition. He *had* said "we." Then her heart picked up its pace as his hand brushed against the nape of her neck. Warmth suffused her, and she was grateful for the dusk. Was he aware of the sensations he caused by just the touch of his hand, just the way he said her name, or the way he looked at her? His profile betrayed nothing. He'd make a great poker player, she thought.

He turned toward her. "What about you? You like kids, don't you? Why didn't you and Mr. Corporate Husband have any of your own?"

Abby bit her lower lip. How did this man manage to touch on every tender spot she thought she'd buried deep under the surface? "He wanted them," she said reluctantly, hoping he'd drop the subject.

"And you didn't?" he asked incredulously. "What about teaching them to ride and making their dreams come true?"

She managed a rueful smile. "I didn't even know how to make my *own* dreams come true, so it's just as well I didn't have any."

"Dreams or kids?"

"Either. I don't know why I'm telling you this, but I tried to get pregnant and couldn't. It was quite a disappointment. *I* was quite a disappointment, in so many ways. Now, can we drop this subject and get back to whatever it was we were talking about?'' Unfortunately she couldn't remember what that was, her mind now filled with the painful memories of the constant taking of her temperature, the endless, humiliating battery of tests she'd undergone, time and again, only to find there was nothing wrong. Nothing and everything.

She stared straight ahead into the darkness, scarcely aware that he'd started the swing with his foot and they were gliding back and forth together in a slow, hypnotic rhythm. He'd draped his arm casually around her shoulders now, his fingers exerting a gentle pressure on her arm, sending waves of heat in the direction of her heart. Her head, which had been leaning on the hard wood of the back of the swing, somehow became pillowed on the hard muscles of his arm.

Exactly how it had happened, she had no idea. One minute they'd been arguing about the ranch as usual and then all of a sudden she was telling him she'd been unable to conceive. The secret she'd never told anyone. Why was it easier to confide in this cowboy, this drifter? Why did it feel so good to have his arm around her, when she knew that someday he'd drift out of her life and take her secret with him? Maybe it was the fact that, right now, at this time in her life, she needed someone to talk to, to lean on, to confide in. She needed Quincy's strength, his comfort and his quiet acceptance of her past failures.

Yes, she needed him and he needed her. He needed this job, a place to stay, until he moved on. It wouldn't be forever. As soon as she could afford to hire some more help, he'd leave. Instinctively she knew that. He was meant for bigger things, bigger jobs, bigger responsibilities. But for the moment . . . she closed her eyes and gave in to the delicious warmth that radiated from his body. And she wondered what she'd do if he pulled her close, so close she could feel the hard planes, the flat stomach, the bones and the muscles that made up the man. What would she do if he kissed her there on the porch, in the darkness, his lips on hers, seeking, finding, taking, giving?

And then it happened, not as she'd imagined, but better. A hundred times better. His broad hands touched her cheekbones, turned her face toward him, hesitating only a second before his lips met hers, just long enough for her to see the stark desire in his eyes. Long enough to feel something inside her let go, something she'd been holding on to for too long.

The first kiss was a test, a light brush of his lips against hers. The second was for real. Real heat, real passion—once simmering, now ready to boil over. When she shifted in the swing to return his kiss, she felt him pull back, a low moan of protest coming from the back of his throat. But before he could change his mind, she wound her arms around his neck, laced her fingers in his dark hair, her mouth moving against his, eager to taste, to explore the man beneath the surface.

Where was the bone-shattering tiredness of a few minutes ago? Replaced by a ferocious energy, a driving desire to take what he had to offer and give it back. He felt so good, his chest pressed against her breasts—so right. The smell of leather and soap and rye grass were all wrapped up in one man, one rugged man, one perfect cowboy. Talk about dreams coming true. He was her dream and her reality. He stopped the swing suddenly with a thrust of his boot against the floor and ran his hands down her back until they rested on the curve of her bottom. "Abby," he said, his voice hoarse.

But she didn't let him speak. His last kiss had just left her breathless and hungry for more. She cupped his face with her hands and brought him with her until her back was flat against the seat and he was lying on top of her.

"Quincy? Abby? That you?" Pop's voice came drifting out of the night air and they both jumped, untangling themselves. Abby quickly stepped to the edge of the porch, inwardly grabbing for composure.

"What is it? Is something wrong?" she asked breathlessly. Quincy was on his feet standing next to her, breathing hard. What would have happened if Pop hadn't come by? Would they be stretched out in the swing by now, tearing each other's clothes off? What had possessed her? She'd lost all sense of time and place.

"Said you wanted to see a calf comin' out," Pop said, leaning against the porch railing.

"I do. Now?" she asked, taking long, slow, deep breaths in an effort to get back to normal. She had a feeling it wouldn't be anytime soon. How long had he been there, and what had he seen?

"Think so."

The three of them started for the barn. "How does it look?" Quincy asked Pop. He'd never been so glad for an interruption in his life. What had he been thinking? He was here for one reason and one reason only. And kissing Abby, becoming involved with her, was *not* it. He yanked his scattered thoughts back to the matter at hand. If there was any danger of this birth not being completely normal, he didn't want Abby around. He couldn't stand to see her disappointed again, to watch the tears run down her face once more. She deserved better than that. She deserved to have her dreams come true, to witness the miracle of birth, to have her own children, to run a successful ranch, even if it wasn't this one.

She certainly didn't deserve him—a man who wanted to see her fail, who was just waiting for her to stumble. A man who would do anything he could to drive her away. Anything but tell her the truth. No, making love to her was not the way to accomplish his goals...or hers. She'd probably realized that by now, too. He stole a sideways glance and saw her profile was just as pure, just as perfect, but maybe just a touch more determined than ever before. Determined to succeed, to let nothing stand in her way. If possible, she probably regretted the episode on the porch more than he did.

He knew better, she didn't. She had no idea what he was doing there. He knew everything about her. Too much. He knew that she'd tried to get pregnant and hadn't. And he knew with certainty that it wasn't her fault, that with the right man... How did he know that? The same way he knew everything, by living close to the earth, with life and death, fertility and infertility all around him, right here on this ranch. He had a second sense about these things, but right now he had to use it for himself. He *couldn't* let himself get involved with Abby. What had just happened on the swing had been a mistake. It couldn't happen again. He wouldn't let it.

"Is it the Brahman you bred with the shorthorn?" he asked Pop.

"That's the one," he said, hobbling behind them.

"I'll take care of it," Quincy replied, putting a hand on Pop's shoulder. "You go to bed."

"You sure?" Pop asked, visibly relieved.

"Sure."

The barn was warm and smelled of hay and warm milk and cows. The Brahman was on her feet, mooing loudly and pawing the ground. Abby stopped suddenly. "Can I call the kids and the parents?"

"This isn't a sideshow," he said, his mouth tightening. Her blue eyes were soft and melting. How could he say no to her? She made him feel like putty. He gave in so fast it made his head spin. "All right."

The smile that lit her face was brighter than the fluorescent lights hanging in the middle of the ceiling and lending an eerie blue quality to the air. He couldn't help grinning back. They both knew she didn't need his permission, but apparently it had been important to her he give his consent. Steeling himself against the odd warmth in the region of his heart, he watched as she backed out of the barn as if she was afraid she might miss something.

Snap out of it, cowboy, he chastised himself. Quickly, he brought a stool over to the cow and eased himself onto it so he could examine her. She was straining at even intervals and he breathed a sigh of relief. So far, so good. Even as he watched, ready to intervene if necessary, he saw the small front toes emerging and the encasing water bag appear at the end of the birth canal. He looked around. Abby had better hurry or she'd miss all the excitement. This cow wasn't going to wait much longer.

Between contractions, the toes disappeared back inside the cow. With the next contraction, they'd be out again and he wished to hell that Abby would get there. She'd never forgive him if she missed it. In spite of everything, he found himself glancing anxiously at the entrance to the barn, silently urging her to hurry.

Then he heard them come into the barn. When he turned his head he saw kids in pajamas, eyes heavy with sleep, whispering, tiptoeing toward him. Abby sat the kids and their parents on bales of hay, then approached so quietly he didn't know she was there until she crouched down next to him, her shoulder brushing against his.

Her gentle touch and the familiar scent of her hair caused a tightening in his chest. Sharing this birth with her was going to be different than all the others he'd done before. He'd never felt this hushed expectancy, this excitement, before. It was her excitement he was feeling.

As the toes appeared again, he heard Abby gasp. She beckoned to the children and they came forward, crowding close. The nose of the calf had just come into view, snuggled above and between its front toes just as it should be. The kids giggled nervously. Quincy exhaled slowly. At last, a normal delivery. He looked over his shoulder at the parents sitting on the straw, hushed and expectant.

"When's it *all* coming out?" a little boy asked.

"He comes out little by little, jerk by jerk," Quincy explained. "Each time the cow gives a push we'll see a little more of the calf. But it's going to take a while for the whole body to make it through the canal. The cow has to rest between pushes." He gave the animal an encouraging pat on the side, and she mooed loudly.

It would have been easier and quieter without the kids, Quincy thought, but it was nice to see them sitting there, awestruck by the miracle of birth, leaning forward, their eyes as big as horseshoes, waiting, watching....

With each jerk, the calf advanced forward, revealing a pink nose, a smooth forehead and small pink ears. And with each jerk, the kids—and their parents behind them—leaned farther forward to watch the animal come out. It was Abby who leaned the farthest, so close he was afraid she'd fall over. Her eyes glowed the brightest as she watched each motion, every contraction. He could almost feel her holding her breath as the calf's shoulders squeezed through the narrow birth canal, then the chest and the stomach.

"Everything's okay, isn't it?" she breathed in his ear.

"So far, so good," he said, brutally squashing down the rush of heat he experienced at her close whisper. He didn't want to ever promise her anything he couldn't deliver. Not after the last time. He couldn't stand to see the crushing disappointment in her eyes again.

The cow gave her last push. A limp, helpless calf covered in membrane finally lay in Quincy's large hands. With great gentleness, Quincy set the calf on the ground in front of its mother. Abby closed her eyes and felt a tear slide down her cheek.

"It's alive," Quincy assured her.

She opened her eyes and smiled at him. "Thank God." She leaned back on her heels and watched the cow vigorously licking her calf with its big, rough tongue. Quincy told the kids the licking was necessary to remove the sack the calf had spent its last nine months in, to warm and dry its body and, most of all, to let it know that it was cared for. His voice was like smoke, warm and heavy, curling around her and enveloping her. Abby let it. He might think the miracle of birth was just another chore to him, but she knew that he felt the same sense of wonder she did, at least right now.

She could tell by his voice, his almost imperceptible sigh of relief when the calf began to breathe. The children were stretching and yawning and had already wandered off with their parents back to the bunkhouse. Abby knew the work wasn't done yet. She'd read books on calving and she knew. She stood up to get the iodine to cauterize the umbilical cord and the antiseptic soap to wash the cow's udder. But before she could move, the cow began to hum a low, soothing moan to her calf. The vibration of the hum filled the air and shook Abby's whole being.

She looked down into Quincy's eyes and saw that he felt it, too. And while the cow hummed and licked her baby, the calf came to life before their eyes, blinking at them, trying to stand. Abby reached down to help it up, but Quincy pulled her hand away.

"Leave her alone, she has to do it on her own. She doesn't need our help." He squeezed her hand in his and Abby felt a current flow from his body to hers.

She knew he was right, but she couldn't bear to watch the calf struggle to find its mother's teat. She pulled her hand away.

"I'll get the iodine," she said, and went to the medicine chest on the shelf. When she returned, the calf was on its wobbly feet and just ended its search. The loud sucking sounds made Abby's eyes smart with tears. She didn't realize how anxious she'd been until now. Carefully, she washed the cord and then leaned against the wall of the barn, her knees suddenly too weak to support her.

She didn't know why she was so tired. She hadn't done anything. It was the cow who'd done all the work tonight. Quincy looked at her from across the barn, where he was spreading fresh hay in a narrow stall for the cow and its calf.

"Well," he said, "was it everything you thought it would be?"

She nodded, afraid to trust her voice. "Oh, yes, even better."

"Your first time?"

"I've read about it, but it isn't the same."

"No," he agreed, "you have to be there."

"I'm so glad I was."

"Thank Pop for that."

"I will, but I imagine he's gone to bed."

"What you should do."

"Not yet. I'm too...too..." She tore her gaze from the newborn calf and looked at Quincy. How could she put a name to what she was feeling tonight? As if every nerve ending was exposed, leaving her naked and vulnerable. She'd never shared an experience like this with anyone, never felt a bond wrap itself around them like this, her and Quincy. She hadn't known that sharing a miracle made the miracle that much more miraculous.

"Too excited?" he asked from behind the partition to the stall.

"More than that. I'm overwhelmed. I had no idea, did you?" Of course, he did. He'd seen a hundred calves being born, maybe more. She was rambling on, digging herself a hole in an emotional quagmire. No wonder he didn't think she had what it took to run a ranch. She had to get a grip on her emotions. This was her first calving experience, but there'd be many more and Quincy wouldn't always be there. The thought sobered her.

"I'm okay now," she assured him.

He lifted his head above the partition and looked at her.

"I got carried away," she said with an abashed smile. Both here and back there on the swing. She'd been carried away by his lips on hers, the warmth of his body, the taut muscles against her, the urgency in his kiss. "But it won't happen again," she assured him.

"What won't?" He came out from behind the stall and faced her. Something in her tone told him she wasn't just talking about what had taken place in the barn.

"What happened on the swing."

"Why not?"

"Because I'm your boss and you're not going to be around forever. We both know that. I can't afford to get involved with someone like you." She wrapped her arms around her waist to keep from shaking. She didn't want to talk about it, but she had to clear the air between them, to make sure it didn't happen again.

He nodded slowly as her words sank in. Of course she couldn't afford to get involved with him. Then why did her words cause a shaft of pain to shoot through him? She was only stating the obvious. "You're absolutely right," he heard himself reply. What else could he say?

She bit her lip. Somehow, she hadn't thought he'd agree so readily. "I don't know anything about you," she said more to convince herself than him. She knew how his skin felt against hers, how warm and insistent his lips were, how rough and gentle his hands could be, but she didn't know why he was here, working for her, when it was clear he didn't want to work for anyone.

"Right again," he agreed, his lips numb, his brain on automatic. How could she say she didn't know anything about him? They'd spent the better part of these past weeks together, working, eating, sharing, talking....

"If everything's under control, then," she said, "I think I'll go to bed."

"Everything's under control," he said, and she knew he was speaking about more than the newborn calf and her mother. He'd been in control since the first day he'd arrived. She only wished she could say the same for herself.

The first thing she did was to get up at dawn and cook a hearty breakfast for her hands and her guests—Western omelets and sugar-cured ham. Pop told her Quincy had been up all night, as four new calves had been born. She wished she'd been there with him, watching the little toes coming out first. She could have helped. She might even have delivered one by herself.

He'd said everything was under control, and it probably had been, but she should have been there, anyway. She shouldn't have gone to bed. She hadn't been able to sleep, anyway. She didn't quite have her emotions under control the way Quincy obviously did. Not yet. But she was getting there. She looked around the dining-room table at the guests, who were busy spreading homemade strawberry jam on hot biscuits, and congratulated herself on not thinking about Quincy—not much, anyway.

After breakfast she announced the day's activities and led the kids out to gather eggs and feed the chickens. Then she sent them off on a treasure hunt to look for such things as bluebells, prairie larkspur and cord grass. She smiled to herself as they left and she returned to the house. It was such a pleasure to share the beauty of this land with others, to introduce children to nature. This was what it was all about. *This* was what she'd had in mind when she'd bought the place.

Quincy watched her through the kitchen window. He'd just filled his plate with a wedge of omelet and was standing at the window, plate in one hand, fork in the other, when she'd rounded the corner, a smile on her face, the sun turning her hair to molten gold. Damn. If only she weren't so sensitive, so vulnerable, so...beautiful. If only she didn't love the ranch. He'd been skeptical the first time she'd said it, but he couldn't deny it anymore. She loved it.

So what? he asked himself, turning his back to the window. He loved it more, had loved it longer. It was merely time to make plans, contingency plans. Just in case. In case the cows all got born, grew up and got sold. In case the guests all had a good time, went home happy and told all their friends about it. In case she started making money, started on that road to real success with her venture...and his ranch.

In case she found out who he was and why he was there. In case he found himself weakening. Yes, now was the time for some serious planning. Now, before it was too late. He had to take steps to make sure she didn't succeed. Of course, there was no need to actually destroy her confidence, just shake it enough to make her want to sell him back his ranch, make her happy to let go of it. Make her realize her place wasn't really here, after all. If he was careful, he could even work it so that she was grateful to *him* for taking it off her hands. And one of the things he could do was be sure to emphasize how the ranch, and its day-to-day operation, needs and disasters, was anything but fun. Ranches weren't supposed to be fun, anyway, they were hard work. He had a feeling Abby hadn't really been introduced to that concept yet.

He took a break from calving. After he'd eaten his breakfast, he made sure Rocky and Curly would tend to the pregnant cows, and saddled Magic, riding out as far as he could and still be on Bar Z land. He carried fence wire coiled on the back of his saddle. Abby had asked him once to check on some broken fence. It was good to get away from the barn and the guests.

Out there by himself, he came to the realization that he'd been helping the guests have a good time and it was time he stopped being so helpful. It was hard to say no to kids, especially when they looked at you as if you were a superhero. It was hard to say no to Abby, too, when she looked at him with those big, blue eyes. But he had to stop being Mr. Nice Guy and pursue his goal with more single-minded determination.

After he got back to the ranch, he fed and watered Magic, then took the long, scenic route to the house, passing the pump house. He paused before he opened the door and stared at the ancient old pump. If it were *his* ranch he'd order a new one, but when he'd asked Abby she'd said she couldn't afford it. One of these days it was going to run dry and burn out the seals— *One of these days....* Why not today or tomorrow?

Grinning, he reached down and opened the drain valve. The water began to trickle out slowly. It might take a few hours, it might take all night, but the next time the water in the tank dropped and the pump started, it would burn out. Of course it could be fixed, but it would be his recommendation, naturally, that she get a new one. This time he would offer to pay for it. But then there would be a delay and some inconvenience. He was counting on the inconvenience. Up to now things had been too convenient. And that was his fault. Closing the door of the pump house behind him and walking away, he also closed the door on the little voice in his conscience that told him he'd just made a big mistake. As he turned and walked back to the house, the sound of running water faded in the distance.

When he'd washed up and changed his shirt, he found a sign on the kitchen door that announced a wienie roast down by the creek instead of dinner. He scowled to himself. He didn't want to mix with single parents or their kids tonight. He especially didn't want to mix with Abby. He didn't want to see her interacting with her guests, laughing, talking, and making sure they were having a good time. Not after what he'd just done.

But he was hungry, so he ambled in the direction of the creek, toward the place where the creek widened to what used to be the old swimming hole. He heard voices and then he saw Abby behind a grill, turning hot dogs with a smile on her face for the kids who were waiting patiently, paper plates in hand.

He stalled as long as he could, staying away from the grill and avoiding her gaze, getting the latest on the cattle and the status of the newborns from Pop and Curly and Rocky. They urged him to get over to the picnic table and fill his plate.

"Potato salad's great," Curly announced, stabbing a large chunk with his fork.

"Don't miss the baked beans," Rocky advised.

"And the homemade relish," Pop enthused.

Quincy edged over to the picnic table. Out of the corner of his eye he saw Abby moving in his direction, tongs in hand.

"I was afraid you'd miss the picnic," she said. "Nobody knew where you were."

"I was out mending the fences. We wouldn't want any cows to escape," he said, his eyes on his plate.

"Well, I'm glad you made it back in time."

He nodded and found he couldn't avoid her gaze any longer. Her eyes were wide and soft. She smiled, and her lips parted slightly, reminding him suddenly of how she kissed with a hunger that made him think she'd been deprived for too long. With an enthusiasm that shouted there was no to-morrow....

But here it was tomorrow and he'd been doing his damnedest to forget about how she kissed and how she felt in his arms. It wasn't working. He grimaced at the thought. She'd probably forgotten he'd even touched her. Why couldn't he? She'd admitted that she'd gotten carried away and he had agreed. That was supposed to be the end of it. She didn't want to get involved with someone who was just passing through. If only she knew that passing through was the furthest thing from his mind. He didn't realize he'd been staring at her mouth, until she spoke.

"What is it?" she asked.

"Catsup," he said quickly, taking his handkerchief from his pocket and dabbing clumsily at the corner of her mouth. Her lips trembled and he swallowed hard. Why did she have to turn vulnerable on him? Just when he was thinking how gutsy and independent she was, she did something like this. The truth was, she was an irresistible combination of soft and hard, of sweet and sour and tough and tender. Only he had to find the strength to resist the combination. It was getting harder by the day. Which was another reason he had to speed up the process. He couldn't wait any longer for events to take their toll, his emotions were getting tangled up already.

He *wasn't* sorry he'd drained the pump, he told himself quietly. And he didn't feel sorry for her, knowing that to-morrow she wouldn't have anything to smile about as she scrambled to find water for thirsty guests. He only wished the thought of her unhappiness wasn't so hard to swallow.

He carried his full plate to the creek's edge to escape any further conversation, but she followed him. What was wrong with her? Hadn't she told him that she was the owner and he was the cowboy and never the twain should meet? Dusk was falling over the shallow banks of the clear little stream, smoke from the grill drifted their way and in the distance Curly was playing songs on his harmonica. The at-mosphere was too darned romantic for his peace of mind.

"Pretty spot," he remarked as she came and stood next to him. Thankfully his tone carried no indication of his thoughts. He could only hope she'd say "hi," then take her warm eyes and tempting lips back to her guests and out of temptation's reach.

"Isn't it?" she enthused, and pointed to a strong, tall oak by the edge of the water. "Can't you just see the kids jumping into the creek from that tree this summer?"

"You're having more kids here this summer?"

"Yes. There's Family Week in June, right after City Slicker's Week."

"I hope you haven't left anyone out. What about Volvo Owner's Week and Parents Of Only Children?" he asked, mock concern in his voice.

"You're making fun of me," she said, but one corner of her mouth quirked up in amusement.

He felt a grin tug at his own lips. "Whatever gave you that idea?"

"You think I'm hopelessly naive, don't you? But wait till I tell you that Mountain Bike Week is completely booked up."

"I hope that's not the same week we're branding," he said, suddenly serious.

"*I* hope it is, they'll love it."

He shook his head and told himself to be patient. No matter if or *how* much her guests loved the ranch, they wouldn't love it without water for their showers, water in their drinking glasses and water to flush their toilets.

"I don't want guests anywhere near those hot irons and cattle," he said grimly. The kinds of disasters *they* could cook up were definitely not on his agenda. He wouldn't allow anyone, even the livestock, to get hurt.

"We'll talk about it later," she said. "We've got plenty of time." And before he could answer, she'd walked back to the picnic, leaving him to finish his dinner . . . alone. He almost shouted, *Oh, no, we don't. We don't have much time, because before you know it, this ranch is going to be what it was meant to be. A cattle ranch. With no guests.*

Chapter Six

That evening, Pop suggested once again that Quincy move into the ranch house. Quincy would have protested, but he sensed that Pop was getting tired of having him take up space in the middle of his floor. The older ranch hand said he'd checked it out with Abby and she had assured him it was fine with her. So Quincy hauled his duffel bag to the room behind the kitchen, set his leather shaving bag in the small, adjoining bathroom and then pulled back the plaid bedspread on the narrow bed.

To his surprise he found fresh sheets smelling of sunshine, and a big fluffy pillow that seemed out of character for the former occupant of these quarters. He felt a pang of guilt just thinking of Abby making up his bed while he was sabotaging her water system, but, then, this was probably the first of many pangs. He would have to get used to it. Despite the comfort of a bed as compared to a sleeping bag on the floor, Quincy didn't sleep well that night. Memories of warm kisses and sweet-scented hair kept him awake. He also kept wondering when and how she'd find out. He didn't have to wonder long.

It was barely dawn when she knocked on his door.

"Quincy?" Her voice was just above a whisper. He raised his head from the pillow to see her standing in the doorway, a pink, plush bathrobe wrapped around her. Her hair was gathered together in one long braid over one shoulder, like some old-fashioned woman in a Western movie. But there was nothing old-fashioned about her long-legged, curvaceous body, barely concealed by the robe. Her skin was as rosy and delicate as the dawn outside his window. At the deep V of the opening, a cotton camisole was just visible. *Damn.*

"What?" he said, rubbing his forehead.

"Something's wrong. There's no running water."

He threw back the blankets, forgetting he was only wearing boxer shorts, forgetting he wasn't at Pop's anymore. She jerked her head toward the window to avert her gaze while he pulled on a pair of jeans.

"Could be the pump. Didn't I tell you you needed to replace it?"

"Did you?" She caught her lower lip in her teeth. That was all she needed, a big expense. Just when she thought she'd break even this month. There were so many things he'd told her to replace or repair, she couldn't possibly do them all. On the other hand, this *was* important. They couldn't manage without water. She was worried, but not so worried she hadn't noticed his broad bare chest and the washboard stomach, the line where his shorts met his thighs. Her heart pounded and she pretended interest in the fence posts on the horizon.

He was in superb condition. Well, what did she expect from the ultimate cowboy, a paunch, an ounce of fat anywhere? Not a chance. Actually, he wasn't perfect—his hair was standing straight up on top of his head. But that only made her want to smooth it back with her fingers. And his jaw was lined with the shadow of a beard, but that, too, only added to his rugged good looks. It only made her want to rub her cheek across it, to see how it felt. She could feel herself blushing and inwardly kicked herself. If only she hadn't come into the room. If only she'd knocked and then waited in the kitchen instead of standing there listening to the sound of his zipper being zipped, to the whisper of flannel against bare skin.

She continued to stare out the window at dirt and posts as if they were the most fascinating objects in the world. But her mouth was dry, her lips, too. Wryly, she told herself she'd better get used to it. There was no water. And no relief in sight.

The least she could have done was get dressed before she came down. Sighing, she faced facts. It was too late now. She was standing in his bedroom waiting for him to get dressed. He put his shoes on and brushed past her on his way out the door.

"I'm going, too," she said, breaking out of the daze she'd been in.

"You're not dressed," he said with a glance over his shoulder.

"I don't think we'll see anyone we know."

"Suit yourself," he said.

"I will," she said, taking two steps for every one of his, trying to keep up with him as he charged down the path.

He swung the door to the pump house open and she heard the loud whirring of the pump. She reached down to touch it and jerked her hand back. "It's hot," she said.

"It's run dry," he explained.

Abby pulled her robe tightly around herself as if for protection against the bad news. "I should have bought a new one like you said."

"Don't blame yourself."

"Who should I blame?"

"No one. Things break. Things wear out." Keeping his face neutral, he blocked out the worry and self-anger in her tone, busying himself with checking parts of the pump he knew weren't the problem.

"Can you fix it?"

"I can order a new impeller seal."

"Order? How long will that take?"

"Depends," he said, straightening up.

She buried her face in her hands. No water. No showers, toilets, cooking, drinking— "What will we do?"

He shrugged. "You'll think of something."

She looked up. The expression in his gray eyes told her nothing. But he was right, she *would* think of something. There was water in the tank on the tower above them. There was water in the creek. She just had to think of a way to get it to the house, to the kitchen and the bunkhouse. She pressed her lips together and took a deep breath. It was obvious he wasn't going to do anything beyond ordering a new part. And that was fine with her. It wasn't his job. Besides, hadn't she complained that he did too much. Well, this was definitely her jurisdiction.

"See you later," she said, and turned on the heel of her pink bunny slippers. Leaving him in the pump house, she strode down the dusty path toward the bunkhouse, where the guests slept blissfully, unaware that there would be no showers that morning.

Quincy studiously avoided Abby and her guests that morning. After he called in the order for the new pump, which he intended to pay for himself, he retreated to the barn and checked calves for signs of discomfort or disease, cleaned udders, installed a heat lamp here, replaced wet straw there. He hesitated before going in for lunch, then admitted he *was* curious about how Abby was going to solve her problem, and besides, he was hungry.

At first glance everything seemed normal. The boys and Pop were already in place at the table, shaking Parmesan cheese into huge bowls of minestrone soup. Quincy stopped by the stove and ladled himself a bowl, inhaling the rich smell of tomatoes, noodles, beans and broth. Then he looked to the left. Instead of a neat, tidy drainboard, there was a pile of dirty dishes. A half days' worth of them were already stacked, waiting to be washed. He clenched his jaw. Maybe coming in here wasn't such a hot idea, after all. If he was very lucky, he might get out of there before Abby came in. Sure he wanted to see her guests suffer, at least enough so they'd go home and stay there. But he didn't want to see *her* suffer. Telling himself not to be a coward, he moved to the table. If he could handle wartime duty, then he could handle this.

Pop raised an eyebrow as Quincy took his seat. "Ya hear about the pump runnin' dry?"

He nodded. "I ordered a new one from Granger's this morning. Should be in by Wednesday. They'll call."

"Didja tell 'em it was an emergency?"

"Is it?"

Pop frowned. "What'd you expect 'em to do, take a bath in the creek?"

"What about the spa?" Quincy asked, watching the steam rise from his soup.

Pop nodded. "I guess they already thought of that. I seen five kids in it this mornin'. *My* spa."

"Abby will think of something. She's smart."

"She already has," Curly offered. "They're having a water brigade this afternoon, kids, parents, everybody. Said we was free to join in if we wanted."

"We've got work to do," Quincy said shortly. He hoped none of them fell for that old trick, making work seem like fun. He'd give them a few days and then see how much fun they were having.

But later that afternoon he decided to see for himself. He followed the sound of their voices and laughter back down to the creek.

There he found the so-called bucket brigade. Kids, parents and Abby had formed a line. The first person dipped a bucket into the river, then passed it on until it reached the last person who would throw the water into a fifty-gallon drum in the back of the pickup. Quincy peered into one of the drums. By nighttime they might have them all filled. And then what? Haul them to the house, heat the water on the stove and pour it over themselves in the shower? He didn't think so.

This Huck Finn, Tom Sawyer sort of plan, of luring people to do the job for themselves, couldn't last. But it did.

Somehow the guests did it. Shamelessly, he listened in on their dinner conversation for the next two nights...and he never heard one complaint. Instead he heard them animatedly describe how they'd done it, hauled water just like their ancestors. The second night he watched Abby refill the gravy bowl at the stove and admitted to himself that she'd surpassed his wildest expectations.

She caught his eye and gave him a triumphant smile, then turned and went back to the dining room. He tried to ignore a pang of renewed guilt and loneliness. He hadn't spoken to her since the morning in the pump house. He'd left her a note, pinned to the kitchen door, about the status of the pump so he knew that she knew, but she'd left no answer for him pinned to his door. He'd looked, but there had been nothing there. It shouldn't have bothered him, but it did.

That night Quincy was up late with a sick calf. When he approached the house, he was surprised to see the lights in the kitchen were still on. Through the window he saw Abby lift a huge vat of hot water from the stove to the sink. Under the ceiling light he could see that every surface, countertop, chopping block and table of the kitchen was covered with dirty dishes, pots and pans. He saw Abby step back from the sink and look around the room. The dismay on her face was unmistakable. Her shoulders slumped, the corners of her mouth turned down and even from his vantage point, he could see that her eyes were glazed with fatigue.

Startled, she looked up when he opened the door. "I didn't know you were out," she said.

"What are you doing?" he asked idiotically, unable to stop himself. Any fool could see what she was doing. He just didn't know what else to say.

She waved her hand at the pots and pans, dishes and bowls, silverware, cups and saucers. "Just tidying up a little," she said with a wry smile.

"Need some help?" Another stupid question.

She hesitated, twisting a dishrag around in her fingers. He knew how proud she was, how much it would cost her to admit she needed help or that she was tired and that it was more work than one person could possibly do.

He reached for a dish towel. He wouldn't give her the opportunity to turn him down. "Wash or dry?" he asked.

"Wash," she said, a note of relief in the casual, short reply. And that was all she said for a long time. She turned back to the sink and poured hot water into the dishpan, added detergent and began to wash dishes. He rinsed, he dried, and he put away. If she wondered how he knew where things went, she didn't ask. She must be beyond wondering, beyond caring. She must be exhausted. And it didn't make him feel very good knowing *he* was the cause of her fatigue.

But he didn't realize how tired she was until the last dish was washed, rinsed and put away and he saw her rub her forehead with the back of her hand. She leaned back against the sink and opened her mouth to speak.

He covered it with his hand. "Don't thank me," he warned.

"Why not?' she mumbled, her lips warm and soft against his palm.

"Because."

She turned her face to one side and his hand fell to her shoulder. "Can I say just one thing?" she asked.

"As long as it isn't 'thank you.'"

"You're not the big, bad guy you pretend to be."

"Yes I am," he said quietly. Why deny it? She was going to find out someday, anyway.

"Don't worry, I'm not going to tell anybody you do dishes," she assured him, a gleam coming into her weary eyes.

He narrowed his own with mock menace. "You'd better not."

She ran her hand over the small of her back and winced.

"What's wrong?" he asked.

"Nothing." She grimaced at the pain in her body. What a day.

"Too much lifting. Turn around."

Reacting automatically to the gentle yet firm command in his voice, she obediently turned and he ran his hand down her spine until it rested on the curve of her bottom. Her eyes, which had been drooping, flew wide open. His hand was warm and felt wonderful.

"Here?" he asked, exerting a slight pressure.

"Higher," she squeaked, unable to break away.

He moved his hand, then gently kneaded his palm into the curve of her back until she found herself leaning into his hand and moaning softly.

"I think you'd better lie down," he said gruffly, running his hand up her back. Feeling her tremble, a rush of sympathy and admiration for her filled his mind. And then something else—white-hot desire—shot through him and shook him to the bottom of his boots. He didn't want to stop touching her, wanted, in fact, to go with her to that bedroom and lie down and— He pulled his hand away as if he'd been burned.

"You're right," she agreed, turning around, but her eyes were a little too bright, her smile a little lopsided. Had she felt the need for her in his touch?

"I mean, you'd better lie down while I massage your back. You've got some real tension there." Visions of her lying across her ruffled bed tormented him. He told himself to let her go to bed, alone, now. He told himself there was no way he could do what he wanted to do.

"I don't think so," she protested weakly, looking at him from under long lashes.

"Don't worry," he said, more to himself than to her, "I know what I'm doing. I've had experience with this kind of thing."

"I can tell," she murmured. Moving out of the kitchen she flicked the light switch and then opened the door to the dining room. He followed her through the room to the staircase. She hadn't said yes, but she hadn't said no, either. Was he actually going to follow her up the stairs and was she really going to lie down on that fluffy comforter and let him massage her back? Either the stairs were getting steeper or he was hyperventilating just thinking about it.

His thoughts ran heatedly through his mind, so fast he could barely make sense of them. Whatever happened, he wasn't going to take advantage of her. Not take advantage of her? He'd been taking advantage of her from the first minute he'd seen her, advantage of her good nature, her innate kindness, and her charity. But that had never been his intention. He'd never wanted to take advantage of anyone. All he'd wanted was his ranch back. And as soon as he got it, everything would be back to normal.

She'd find out how rotten he really was, and he'd never get involved with another woman as long as he lived. He *couldn't* get along with women. They baffled him, then they bothered him, and then they left him. This time he was prepared. But first there was the matter of her aching body and what he was going to do about it. Perspiration broke out on his forehead as he watched her going up the stairs before him. How had he gotten himself into this?

Entering her bedroom ahead of him, she staggered across the blue-and-brown braid rug and flung herself facedown under the canopy of her bed, her arms over her head. He stood in the doorway, momentarily frozen, clenching his hands at his sides, looking at her. If he left now, she might fall asleep, forget all about her aches and pains, and forget all about him, too. He rocked back on his heels, trying to decide what to do and wondering why the decision wasn't as easy as it should be.

He knew what he wanted to do. He knew what he was aching to do. But that was out of the question. Moving forward, he looked down at her tangled blond hair covering one shoulder, her rib-hugging shirt and the rounded curves of her hips, and he willed himself to be strong. Then he lowered himself to the edge of her bed. Just a few strokes to relax her, to soothe the muscles, to relieve the ache, he assured himself. It was the least he owed her after what he'd done. What he'd do about his own ache had to be postponed...forever.

He started with her shoulders, kneading the knots out of the muscles there. She turned her head to one side and gave a deep, contented sigh that reverberated through her body. He moved down the ridge of her spine slowly, carefully, until he stopped at the hooks of her bra. Without skipping a beat, he reached under her shirt, slid his hands across her smooth skin and unfastened it as if he'd done it a hundred times.

She was holding her breath. He felt it. He heard her stop breathing. When he continued as if nothing had happened, she breathed normally again, slowly, evenly. His hands continued their exploration into the hills and valleys of her anatomy. Little murmurs of pleasure came from her lips, making him imagine how she'd react to full-fledged lovemaking. He closed his eyes. His self-control was close to snapping. Just a few more strokes and he'd have to leave. But a few more strokes on the firm flesh of her rounded bottom and he'd be beyond stopping. Desire surged through him and he pulled himself off the bed while he still could.

She groaned a brief protest. He stopped in the doorway, but she didn't move or make any further sounds. She just made a long, contented sound—like the purring of a kitten—that made him ache all the more...and then fell asleep.

The next morning, Abby saw that Quincy wasn't at breakfast. She stood at the kitchen window, staring out at the driveway where his truck was usually parked and wondering if he'd gone for good. Her mouth tightened. If he had, she'd manage. She'd managed before he came and she'd get along after he'd gone. She had always known he'd go sooner or later. Besides, after last night, maybe it was better he go sooner.

She only had to close her eyes to feel his hands on her body again, his strong capable fingers rubbing away the tension and strain of the day, replacing it with new feelings, a different kind of tension. She fried bacon, she baked muffins, she said good morning to Curly and Rocky and she heated water that she'd hauled for coffee. And all the while she wondered what would have happened if he hadn't stopped after he'd unhooked her bra and freed her breasts. What if she'd rolled over and raised her head to meet his, face to face?

She gave a little shiver and jumped when Pop shouted that the water had boiled over and the muffins were burning. She thanked him with an absent nod and went back to staring out the window. Steadfastly, she ignored the lump in her throat at the thought of Quincy's being gone. If he'd left, she'd have to fix the pump herself. No reason why she couldn't. There had to be a manual somewhere. But first she'd need the part he'd ordered.

After breakfast, she called the hardware store in town. The clerk said Quincy had already been there and picked up the new pump. A strange mixture of elation and relief poured through her at the news that Quincy hadn't left, after all. Then it was replaced, a microsecond later, with a start. New pump? She'd never okayed such a big purchase. He'd said a part, then he'd gone and bought the whole thing. So he hadn't changed, after all. He was still determined to do things his way.

She asked Curly and Rocky to take the guests on a horseback ride, then she went to the barn to look at the fresh new calves. It always soothed her spirits to sit down on a pile of hay and put her arms around a warm, soft, cuddly calf. Pressing her cheek into the soft fur of one, she sighed. She should be working on her indignation, but instead she was daydreaming about what might have, could have, happened the night before.

When she didn't see Quincy at lunch, Abby went out to the vegetable garden and pulled weeds with a vigor she didn't know she'd had in her. Why *should* he bother to hurry back with the new pump when this wasn't his ranch? It wasn't *his* guests who were stuck without water. She was working herself into a full-fledged frenzy when she heard a shout from the bunkhouse.

"Water," yelled one of the guests, and waved to Abby from the second floor.

Abby shaded her eyes from the sun. *Water?* How could that be? She wiped the dirt on her hands onto her jeans and headed for the pump house. And there he was, calmly putting the finishing touches on the installation of a shiny, brand new pump.

"What do you think?" he asked, an unmistakable look of pride on his face. "Pretty nice, huh?"

"I thought you were going to buy *a* part . . . an impeller."

"An impeller seal. I was, but I changed my mind. Don't worry. I'm paying for this."

"Don't worry you're paying for it," she repeated. "You're not paying for anything. Not on my ranch."

He tensed. She knew that for some odd reason he hated being reminded whose ranch it was, but she'd had no choice.

"Take it out of my wages," he suggested. It was a not-so-subtle reminder that she wasn't paying him so she had no control over him.

"Why couldn't you at least have asked me, consulted me, before you made such a major purchase?" she asked, growing indignation in her voice.

"I wanted to surprise you."

"You did," she said grimly.

"I thought you'd be glad."

"I'm glad to have the water back."

He smiled smugly. "No more hauling buckets. No more backaches."

She felt the heat flood her face. A reminder that she'd been putty in his hands last night, lying flat on her stomach while he'd rubbed and stroked her into oblivion. She didn't need to be reminded. She'd never forget.

"Thanks for helping me do the dishes," she said adroitly, changing the subject. She wouldn't get anywhere with the pump situation, so she might as well give it up. For now.

"No aftereffects?" he inquired.

She shook her head. Nothing but a lingering desire to repeat the whole incident, to throw herself into his arms, to feel the heat of his hands through her shirt, through the well-worn denim that covered her legs. If he only knew how he made her feel ... Maybe he did know. The look in his eyes told her his memories of last night were as vivid as hers, maybe more so. His gaze heated up and she looked away.

"Have you had lunch?" she asked.

"No. Is there anything left?"

"In the kitchen."

They walked back to the house while she tried to think of something neutral to say. "How do you like your new room?" she said finally.

"Very handy to the kitchen and to the storm cellar."

"I've never been down there."

"Let's hope you never have to. Kansas tornadoes are famous. And this falls right in the season—April, May and June."

She looked up into the clear blue sky and a shiver ran up her spine as she pictured a black, funnel-shaped cloud moving toward her ranch. She didn't know what she'd do if she lost the ranch. It was the only thing she'd ever owned that was all hers and nobody else's. She loved every stalk of grass, every termite-infested board and every weed in her garden.

The week drew to a close and Abby knew the single parents and their children had had a wonderful time. But she didn't know how wonderful until the morning they left and she stood waving and wiping a tear from her eye. Out of the corner of that same eye, however, she saw Quincy leaning against the porch railing, watching her.

"What's wrong?" he asked, tilting his hat back from his head, a piece of grass clamped in his teeth.

"Nothing. These were tears of happiness. I've achieved something, at last."

"What's that, living through another week of catastrophes?" he asked, but his words were softened by a grin.

"Scoff if you like, but I've just realized that this group of people, who didn't know each other before they came to this ranch, formed a bond while they were here, with each other, with me and with the ranch." She turned to face him, her hands on her hips. "And do you know why?" She didn't wait for his answer. "Because the well went dry. Because they had to endure a little hardship. Because they worked together on the bucket brigade." She gave him a satisfied smile. "And *that's* what it's all about."

"What's what all about?" he asked.

"The ranch. That's what it's for, to give people a chance to make new connections, to break out of old patterns and to see the world in a new light."

"I thought it was to raise cattle for profit," he said dryly.

"Of course. That, too. Aren't you happy with the way the calving went?"

"I would have been happier to have a few more hands."

"Next year," she said hopefully.

"If we're still here."

"*I'll* still be here. Nothing could make me leave. Not after this week. You know it would be almost worth inventing a minor disaster if it could bring people together like that. Not that anyone would do such a thing. I mean, enough disasters happen naturally. Oh, well." She rested her elbows on the fence and looked at him. She wished he could share her joy with the way things were. He deserved to. He'd worked hard, he'd played a positive role in helping the guests have a good time. They'd talked about him, admired him and respected him.

If only she could confine her feelings for him to admiration and respect. But somehow he always provided stronger, deeper feelings, sometimes close to rage, sometimes close to a burning, relentless desire. She vowed to keep those feelings under control this next week and in all the weeks to come.

"What next?" he asked, tilting his head to regard her with his level gray gaze and rubbing his palms together.

"Next? So you do care!"

"What makes you say that?" he asked, surprise and an odd note of wariness in his tone.

"I saw you lifting the little kids off their horses. I saw you teaching them to hold their reins and tighten their stirrups. You can't tell me you don't care about my guests, Quincy. But next week you can relax. The group will be completely self-sufficient."

"What are they, Hell's Angels?"

"No, but you're close. Kansas mountain bikers."

"*What?*"

"I did mention them before, so don't act so surprised. And it entails absolutely no work on your part. That's why I didn't go into detail before. Have you heard of Mountain Mike?"

"I don't think so."

"I hadn't, either, until I saw his ad pinned to a bulletin board in town. He comes onto your ranch with a van full of mountain bikes. He outfits everybody, gives lessons in trail riding to those guests who want them, hands out free T-shirts and then off they go, bicycling into the hills on dirt trails or into town to look at the antique shops. What do you think?" she asked breathlessly.

"I'm stupefied," he admitted.

"Come on, I could have sworn it would take more than that to stupefy you." She walked up to him and crossed her arms over her chest, a teasing gleam in her eyes.

"It usually does. I must be slipping."

There was a glimmer of humor in the depths of his smoky gray eyes that encouraged her. He tried so hard to be all true grit. Why was that?

"You're everybody's idea of what a cowboy should be, you know. That's what the guests said. I can't imagine you ever being in the army. Do you ever think about it?"

"I can't think about it. I just have to try to forget about it and move forward."

She was relieved to hear him say so. Someday he'd have his own place, and another wife, someone who wouldn't leave him, maybe even kids to teach to ride... She tried to picture him somewhere else, on another ranch, but she couldn't. Yet she knew he hated working for anyone else, and her in particular, so what else was there?

"That's what you did, isn't it?"

She boosted herself to the top fence rail and sat down on it, swinging her legs. "I don't know," she admitted. "There are times when I think I keep making the same mistakes over and over. Maybe my ex-husband was right and I'll never be good at anything."

"What are you talking about?" Quincy demanded, abruptly moving closer and caging her with his hands against the fence. "You've proved him wrong a *hundred* times over. You're good at riding, you're good at cooking...and...lots of other things."

She looked down at him, feeling a warmth radiate through her body. A warmth that was kindled by the look in his eyes. "You really think so?" she asked.

"Don't take my word for it, ask Pop, ask those guests who just left."

She looked off across the pasture. She could ask Pop and she could ask the guests, but it was Quincy's approval that meant the most to her. Why? Because he was so competent, so self-sufficient and so hard to please. And because she respected his opinion.

But it wasn't good to rely on one man's opinion. She'd sworn that she'd *never* let that happen again. There was only one person she had to please, and that was herself. Tamping down the urge to fish for more reassurance, she jumped down and rubbed her hands together.

"Well," she said briskly, "only twenty-four hours to get ready for the next group. Don't let me keep you from your work."

Slowly Quincy straightened, then backed away from her, his eyes intent on her face. There were questions in his eyes that she couldn't—wouldn't—answer. But before he walked away, she said, "I appreciate everything you did for me in the past week, to make it such a success."

"Forget it," he said, an odd, flat tone to his voice.

"No, I won't forget it. The night you helped me with the dishes..." There was a long silence. He stopped backing away; she held still. The look in his eyes told her he was thinking about what had happened afterward and he knew that she was, too. And they both knew they'd left something unfinished that night.

Chapter Seven

Quincy headed for the barn, then changed his mind and walked in the general direction of Pop's place. He didn't know where to go. It made him uneasy to be thanked just for doing his job. Well, maybe drying dishes wasn't *exactly* his job, and neither was saddling horses for kids, but it still made him uncomfortable. Especially when he knew that he and Abby were actually working at cross-purposes. She didn't know that. She would find out someday, but before that happened he had to make sure she came to the conclusion, in her own good time, that it was not in her best interest to stay on the ranch. Then she would sell it to him and go do something else. He would help her see it as an opportunity and not a personal failure, just a change of direction. Feeling a bit better for that thought, he knocked on Pop's door, walking in when Pop yelled at him to enter.

"Been wantin' to talk to ya," Pop said, sweeping a stack of newspapers off the chair for Quincy.

"About branding?" Quincy asked, taking a seat.

"About Abby."

"What about her?"

"What do ya think of her?"

"She's fine."

"That all?"

"What do you want me to say?"

"I seen ya lookin' at her when she comes into the kitchen at dinnertime."

Quincy shrugged. "Who'm I supposed to look at, you and Curly and Rocky? She's a lot easier on the eyes than any one of you. So what choice do I have?"

"Ya got a choice to move on. Yer not gettin' any richer stayin' here."

"That's true, but if you think I'm staying because I'm interested in Abby, you're wrong."

"Am I?"

Quincy leaned forward in his chair. "Yes, you are."

"Then why are ya stayin'? Refresh my memory."

"I want my ranch back. I thought it would be easy. I'd make her an offer she couldn't refuse. I hadn't counted on her being so...well, you know, like she is. Then I realized it would take a little longer than I'd thought. Besides, it was your idea I stay here. Anyway, I'm waiting."

"For what?"

"For her to get tired of working twenty-four hours a day, doing other people's laundry and making their beds and trying to raise cattle at the same time."

"Yer not comin' on to her, are ya?"

Quincy felt the heat go up the back of his neck. "Why?"

"Because I don't want to see her hurt. She's been hurt bad in the past."

"Did she tell you that?"

"Didn't have to, I guessed."

Quincy's stomach twisted into a knot. He didn't have to guess. He knew. She'd told him all about it. "Let's get something straight," he said gruffly. "You know she doesn't belong on a ranch, don't you?"

"Why not?"

"Because she doesn't know anything about ranching. Don't tell me you haven't noticed."

"She's a fast learner. Give her time."

"I *am* giving her time."

"Time to succeed, not fail."

"Wait a minute," Quincy interjected. "If she succeeds, she won't sell and I don't get my ranch back."

Pop sighed. "That's a problem," he admitted.

"At least we agree on that," Quincy said stiffly. "I never thought you'd take her side in this."

"I'm not takin' sides," the old man said, scratching his head. "Ya both want the same thing, I'm trying to think how ya can get it."

"The ranch, you mean."

"The ranch and...that's not all."

Quincy stretched his long legs out in front of him. "Go ahead. What else?" The old man never ceased to amaze him. He'd been around, seen a lot and forgotten very little. He'd always been generous with advice, but before this, it had always been on the subject of cattle or the ranch, not women.

"I suspect ya both want to settle down again one day, get married again an' have kids," Pop said.

Quincy got to his feet. This was going too far. Pop had gone off the deep end this time, if he was suggesting what Quincy thought he was suggesting.

"Well, you suspect wrong. I know for a fact that Abby isn't interested in getting married again and neither am I. I don't have to explain why, either. You knew Corinne. You know what she did to me. The only thing I'm lacking in this world is..."

"The ranch. I know. Ya told me. But I'm telling ya, you wouldn't be happy here by yourself."

"I'm not going to *be* by myself. I'd have more hands and I'd have you. You're not leaving, are you? If you think I'd be lonely, you're crazy."

Pop grinned. "I been called worse by bigger fools than you, but I don't let that stop me."

Quincy shook his head and heaved a sigh of frustration. What could he say to convince Pop he wasn't interested in

Abby? He sometimes had a hard time convincing himself. He changed the subject to branding and they talked for a few minutes before Quincy left to feed the cattle.

Abby was in the orchard when Pop found her, examining the blooms of a peach tree for signs of disease.

"Ya look mightly pretty standin' there," he observed, taking a seat on the stump of an old walnut tree. "Pretty as a picture."

"Thank you, Pop," she said with a faint smile. "Do you know anything about peach curl?"

"No, but Quincy does."

"Yes," she sighed. "Quincy knows everything."

"Is that bad?" he inquired.

"No, of course not. But it's frustrating to have to depend on him for everything."

"Everythin'? I don't see him doin' no cookin', or balancin' the books, or organizin' activities for the guests."

"That's because he doesn't want the guests here."

"Did he tell ya that?"

"More than once," she said ruefully. "He doesn't think I can do it."

"That bother ya?" Pop asked.

Abby straightened her shoulders and inhaled the smell of the blossoms on the fruit trees. "Of course not. I don't need his approval."

"Maybe he don't approve of ya, but he sure admires ya."

Her cheeks reddened and she pressed a peach leaf between her thumb and forefinger. "Admires me for what?"

"For workin' so hard, for one thing."

"He thinks I'm crazy for working so hard."

"What'd ya think of him?"

"Quincy?" She gazed off at the trees—apple, plum, peach and cherry trees that dotted the orchard—and she narrowed her eyes. "I can't really figure him out. You've known him a long time. What do you think?"

Pop chewed thoughtfully on a blade of grass. "Quincy won't let on, but he's hurtin' inside. When that little war come along he lost everythin', his land and his wife. And ya know what hurt the most?''

Abby nodded. "I know. I can tell by the way he looks at the hills, and the cattle and even the house. He's hungry for his own place.''

Pop nodded vigorously. "Ya got that right.''

"Then why doesn't he go buy a ranch somewhere? He seems to have enough money. He can afford to work for nothing. He bought that pump the other day, out of his own pocket.''

"Did he? Well, far's I can tell, he's just not ready. He doesn't know what it is he really wants. What I think is that he needs a woman as much as you need a man.''

Abby almost laughed out loud, the idea was so preposterous. "I don't think I agree with you there,'' she said.

"Why not?'' Pop asked, the lines that forked off from the corners of his eyes deepening.

Abby leaned back against the smooth bark of the peach tree. "To me, needing someone, relying on someone, especially a man, and especially a husband, is admitting that you can't make it on your own. I was married once, you know that, and I lost every bit of self-confidence I had. I had no money worries, I grant you that, but that's the only good thing I can say about the whole experience. I told myself I'd never let it happen again, Pop. I told Quincy that and I'm telling you that right now.''

"Ya told Quincy you was never gettin' married again?'' Pop asked.

"Yes, and he agreed. It's the one thing we agree on. But if he *is* looking for a woman, he shouldn't have any trouble,'' Abby said, the image of him in his boxer shorts popping out of nowhere. Suddenly she remembered her brief glimpse of his broad chest and washboard stomach. No, he wouldn't have any trouble, at all. Especially if he didn't try to tell them what to do.

It certainly wouldn't bother her if he did find someone. She was totally indifferent to his personal life. But her stomach gave a sudden lurch at the thought of Quincy giving some other woman the benefit of that warm, smoky gaze, of his lips on hers, his hands massaging the small of her back— She forced her gaze back to meet Pop's.

"All the more reason for him to leave this place," she continued. "There's no one for him here."

"Only you," Pop suggested, looking off into space.

"*Me?*" she squeaked. "Quincy and me?" She choked back a laugh. "You must be crazy."

"Guess I must," Pop admitted, getting to his feet. "Yer the second person today that's noticed it. Well, I don't know nothin' about peach curl and ya got yer mind made up on this marriage business, I see. But ya can't say I didn't try."

"No," she said, "I can't." She watched him hobble away slowly, wondering what he was up to. The idea of an old grizzled cowboy like Pop playing matchmaker was unbelievable. Almost as unbelievable as the idea of her and Quincy. She pinched a curled peach leaf and plucked it from the tree. She must have misunderstood.

The bicyclists who arrived the next day were a hardy bunch. And Mountain Bike Mike was everything he advertised himself to be. Affable, enthusiastic and generous with advice and attention to detail. Some of the experienced riders adjusted their goggles, fastened their helmets and sped off to the dirt trails in the hills, becoming only a blur of spandex in the distance. Others set off for town on designated trails along the road, to browse the antique shops.

Abby couldn't believe they'd all disappeared by ten o'clock in the morning. She stood in the driveway next to Mountain Bike Mike and watched them go. She'd packed picnic lunches for them so they wouldn't have to come back until late afternoon. As much as she'd loved sharing the calving with her last guests, she felt a sense of relief knowing she wouldn't have to provide entertainment this week. But she felt an unaccustomed pang of something akin to loneliness as the last guest disappeared from sight.

"It looks like fun," she said with just a trace of wistfulness.

"Give it a try," Mike said, gesturing toward the extra bikes in the back of his van. "You ride, don't you?"

"I haven't ridden a bike since I was a kid," she said as Mike lifted a sturdy mountain bike down onto the gravel driveway for her.

"Know how to shift?" he asked.

She shook her head and Mike spent ten minutes explaining the twelve gears. Fortified with the knowledge, she set off down the driveway, gripping the handlebars tightly and wobbling just slightly. When she reached the end of the driveway, she lifted her hand to give Mike a triumphant wave. But he wasn't looking at her. He was engaged in conversation with Quincy. To her surprise, he was taking another bike from his van and raising the seat as high as it would go to accommodate Quincy's six-foot-three-inch frame. As she stood there, immobilized, she watched Quincy pedal toward her, his forehead creased in concentration.

She hadn't seen him since yesterday, but she'd thought about him. Thought about what Pop had said, about his not-so-subtle suggestion that she and Quincy... Just thinking about it made her face flame with embarrassment. She only hoped he hadn't said something similar to Quincy. She watched him come closer, his eyes on the gearshift.

"Whoa," he called to his bike as he headed straight for Abby. When it didn't respond to his command, he veered off at the last minute and Abby jumped out of the way. He slammed on the hand brakes, which caused him to lurch forward over the handlebars. He got off and looked over at her, an abashed grin on his face.

"Don't tell me there's something *you* can't do," she said in mock surprise.

"Lots of things. Who said I could do everything?" he asked, turning the bike around and giving her a sideways glance.

"I just assumed if you could ride a horse you could ride a bike. Guess I was wrong."

"I just learned one major difference," Quincy said. "Horses respond to commands, bikes don't." His gaze ran over her khaki shorts, her long, smooth legs, then up to her white cotton camp shirt, lingering on the neckline, the patch pockets over her breasts. She felt the heat spread through her body, as if he'd undressed her right there in the driveway.

"Where are you going?" he asked.

"Nowhere. I just came out to see the guests off." She grasped her handlebars and took off back toward the van, allowing the breeze to cool her cheeks and the rest of her body.

He followed her back down the driveway. They got off the bikes and stood awkwardly at the back of the van, looking anywhere but at each other.

"You guys did great," Mike enthused. "But I thought you'd keep going."

"Oh, no," Abby said, yet her gaze strayed to the hills, to the trails that edged the grass, and she wished, just for a moment, that she was a guest and not the host. Wouldn't it be wonderful if *she* could go off on a carefree ride with lunch in her backpack?

"Compliments of the house," Mike said, dusting off the bikes with a chamois cloth. "I won't charge you any rental."

Abby looked at Quincy and Quincy looked at Mike. With an almost imperceptible shrug of the shoulders, he said, "Why not?"

She could think of a million reasons why not, but they never got as far as her lips. Instead she ran into the kitchen and threw together another lunch just like the ones she'd made for the guests. When she returned to the front driveway, Mike was ready with two backpacks. Abby stuffed a large paper sack into her pack and gave Quincy a bottle of mineral water and a bottle of wine.

Then she straddled the bike before she could ask herself what on earth she was doing. It was bad enough taking a day off when she had so much to do, even worse taking a day off with Quincy, the one man she should be avoiding. For all she knew Pop *had* approached Quincy with his suggestions that they needed each other, and he was feeling as uneasy as she was. And now here they were, stuck with each other. On the other hand, *he* was the one who'd said, "Why not?" Not her.

At the end of the driveway, they turned right onto a narrow dirt path. "Where to?" he asked.

"What about the pond?"

He nodded and set off ahead of her. The sun beat down on her head, but the breeze cooled her face as long as they were still on flat land. She kept her eyes on Quincy's back, on his broad shoulders, on his hair that brushed the collar of his blue denim work shirt. It was mesmerizing watching him as she pedaled behind him. He never turned to look at her, but she knew that he was aware she was right behind him.

She forgot about the ranch, about the guests and the cows. Instead she concentrated on shifting gears for the increasing slope of the hills. It occurred to her that she had to keep up with Quincy, but her thighs ached, she was short of breath, and the sweat was pouring down her face. They stopped once and turned to look back at the ranch, spread out like a primitive painting beneath them. There it was: the house, the corral, the barn and the bunkhouse, and the fields of grass, fenced and cross-fenced. She caught her breath at the beauty of the scene. It was all hers, as far as the eye could see—*her* house, *her* barn and *her* fields. She breathed a long sigh of contentment.

"It looks like a painting," she said softly.

"By Grandma Moses," he agreed, leaning against the handlebars of his bike.

She slanted a curious look in his direction.

"What's wrong?" he asked. "Can't cowboys appreciate art?"

"Of course," she said quickly. "I suppose you read poetry, too?"

He grinned. "Anything *but* cowboy poetry, but don't tell anybody." He turned away from her then, and shaded his

eyes to survey the panorama spread out in front of them.
She took the opportunity to study his profile, all lines and
angles. Quincy was like a painting himself. Granted, *she* was
no artist, but her fingers itched for paint and brushes. How
else could she capture the bronze of his skin, the hollows of
his cheeks, the sensuous thrust of his lower lip? She supposed, short of painting him, that the only real way to hold
on to his image was to engrave it in her mind. An odd pang
went through her at the thought. What was wrong with her?

"Ready?" he asked, putting his hat on.

Shaking her head to get rid of her strange melancholy,
Abby plastered a smile on her face and followed Quincy.
They continued single file on the narrow rutted path, going
past the one and only ranch bull, and then past fields of
larkspur, startling prairie chickens who scurried and
swooped among the vast stands of cord grass and wild rye.
The smell of the virgin tall grass invaded Abby's senses,
filling her with a feeling of oneness with the land...and with
the man who rode with her.

Once in the groove of rhythmic pedaling, she forgot how
tired she was, forgot how many miles they'd ridden, forgot
even that her legs were trembling with fatigue. But when the
pond suddenly appeared in the distance like a shimmering
mirage, she almost toppled off her bike in relief. Stopping,
she let the bike fall over in the grass and watched content-
edly as Quincy opened the mineral water and handed the
bottle to her. She drank deeply, then handed it back to him.

Quincy drank from the plastic bottle, tasting her lips. He
could have sworn the imprint of her mouth was still on the
rim and the mere thought of such a thing made his mouth
go dry. Trying to be casual, he glanced at her as he drank.
A bead of perspiration had trickled down her chest and was
disappearing into the hollow between her breasts. His heart,
already beating fast from the uphill climb, shifted into
overdrive. He tried to look away but he couldn't. She was
pink-cheeked and winded, her hair whipped into a golden
tangle around her face.

"We made it," she said delightedly, holding her arms out to the sky, the grass and the blue waters of the pond. He drank some more water and tamped down his own reaction to her natural exuberance. He wanted to grab her, to see if her heart was beating as fast as his. He wanted to feel her silky hair against his cheek, and taste her lips on his—

But that was no way to convince himself that he had no interest in Abby other than taking the ranch away from her. And that was very important, indeed. Because if *he* didn't believe it, how could he expect to convince someone else, like Pop?

No, he thought as he followed her down to the edge of the pond, she was just another woman, a little prettier maybe, a little harder working, a little more desirable than most even. So desirable he had to keep his hands clenched around the water bottle to keep from putting his hands on her shoulders and turning her around so he could kiss her. But that, he told his aching body, was it. Any kiss now would just be a way of congratulating her for making it to the top. But it wasn't something he could indulge in. He knew from experience that one of Abby's kisses was like one of her hot biscuits in the morning. One was never enough, and they just left you hungry for more.

Just as he was reinforcing his rapidly eroding self-control, Abby turned on the heel of her canvas sneakers and stopped abruptly, her face only inches from his.

"Have you been here before?" she asked, a faint, puzzled look in her sky blue eyes.

"Here?" he asked, taking a step backward. He'd been here a hundred times. It was one of his favorite places, for fishing or just thinking. But, then, that was the trouble with lying. You could never remember what you'd said when you most needed to.

"Did I say I'd been here before?"

"I thought you did."

"Oh. Well, I didn't... I, uh, haven't—been here before, that is," he said, meeting her gaze. That was another thing about lying. You had to look people straight in the eye while you did it. Trouble was, her gaze was so blue, so earnest, he wondered how much longer he could go on like this without cracking under the strain. Suddenly he knew he had to do something to bring matters to a head, to solve the problem of his ranch/her ranch. Which meant he would have to increase the pressure on her. The pump problem had been a good idea, but it had backfired. The next time he would have to be more careful.

If only she didn't see this land as some kind of paradise. He'd seen the look in her eyes as she gazed at it back there, when it had been spread out in front of them. He'd known what she was thinking before she'd said it, because he felt the same way. But, darn it, shouldn't it count any that *he'd* felt that way longer, stronger, than she had?

His ancestors had been riding the Flint Hills for three generations, while she was essentially a city girl, playing at ranching. All right, fine, maybe not exactly playing at it. She was working at it, and working hard. But that didn't mean she deserved the ranch, *his* ranch.

Abruptly, he put his hands on her shoulders and turned her around, so he wouldn't have to look into those trusting blues anymore. "Let's go," he said flatly. "I'm hungry."

He watched as she agreeably began moving, looking for a likely spot for their picnic. He watched her backpack bounce against her back, watched her hips sway just slightly, a few steps in front of him, and wished he could turn her around again and kiss away her doubts about him. But then, that wouldn't be fair, would it? He knew too much about her, knew how vulnerable she'd been since her divorce, how distrustful of men. Even Pop knew how she'd been hurt in the past. And then, of course, there was the little fact that she knew nothing about him. But what if he told her everything? Right here and now, right there at the edge of the pond, surrounded by water and sun and tall grass—

He could picture the look in her eyes, the hurt, the shock. He shut down the thought immediately. What good would it do? He would have to leave and then he'd never get his ranch back, not even if the bank foreclosed. She'd never sell it back to him. And then where would he be? No. He would just have to be patient a little longer, and hope that things went his way.

She stopped at the edge of the water and swung her backpack down onto the ground. Deftly she spread a checkered cloth on the grass and covered it with plastic containers, paper cups and plastic utensils. While he poured them each a paper cup of white wine, she spooned heaping portions of chicken salad, cold asparagus spears and crisp bread sticks onto each plate.

She added two cloth napkins to the spread, then looked up at him. He handed her a cup of wine and lightly touched it with his. She sat down.

"To Grandma Moses," he said. "If only she were here to do justice to this scene." He meant it. Abby's hair gleamed gold in the bright sunlight, her eyes shimmered like the waters in the pond. Yet somewhere inside he admitted the truth—no painting would do her justice. So he found himself staring at her, trying to memorize the curve of her cheek, the line of her chin, the way her long legs stretched out in front of her.

"I'm afraid she wouldn't have survived the climb," Abby said as Quincy sat down opposite her. "I had some doubts about it myself."

"Not you," he said teasingly, biting into a crisp sesame seed bread stick.

"I'm not in as good shape as you," she said, laughing.

"Your shape looks good to me." He couldn't resist. This time he let himself take one more look at her full breasts, imagining the sheen of perspiration clinging to them, imagining how they'd feel with his hands cupped around them. A rush of hormones shook him and threatened to engulf him in desire.

Abby shifted away from the edge of the checkered tablecloth, only too aware of his heated gaze. Slightly embarrassed, she felt her breasts strain the confines of her wispy silk bra, the tips growing hard and sensitive. Maybe Pop was right. She needed a man, and Quincy needed a woman. So why didn't he go off and find one? Anyone but her. She willed herself to breathe slowly, normally. If she did need a man, she needed self-reliance more. She had no time for relationships. Finally she spoke.

"What are you doing here, anyway?"

His gaze traveled lazily from the curves of her breasts to her hips and down her bare legs. She felt as if he'd caressed her everywhere he looked. The air hummed and shimmered between them, bees buzzed and the pond lapped at their feet, but she was barely conscious of any of it. Her question went beyond this afternoon's unexpected bike ride, and his answer was important.

"I just came along for the ride," he said at last, grinning easily.

"That's what I thought." Releasing the breath even she hadn't been aware she'd been holding, Abby congratulated herself on her great instincts. Ignoring the stab of regret in her ungrateful heart, she hardened her resolve. She had no intention of getting involved with some man who was just along for the ride. She couldn't afford to get involved with any man at all. So why had she ridden miles, uphill, to have lunch with a man whose mere gaze could make her melt inside and whose touch she avoided like the devil because it could set her on fire? Because she'd lost her mind. But only momentarily. Any minute now she'd get it back. She took a sip of wine. He did the same.

She picked up her fork and delved into her chicken salad. If she acted normal on the outside, maybe she'd begin to feel normal on the inside. But instead, the sun and the wine and the food soon made her feel fuzzy around the edges, inside and outside. She stared at the blue waters that rippled in the pond. The sun was too bright. She lay back on the grass and closed her eyes, feeling the blades tickle the back of her knees and the sensitive skin along her inner thighs. She clutched the paper cup in her hand.

"More wine?" he asked.

She shook her head, and watched dazedly as he came closer. The earth trembled, and vibrations filled the air as he bent over to take her cup out of her hand. Their hands met. His fingers were wide, warm, slightly rough to the touch. His thumb caressed her palm and she exhaled a ragged sigh. She gripped his hand and held on tight to stop the spinning, the dizziness. She shut her eyes, but the sensations only increased in direct proportion to the nearness of Quincy. And he was getting *very* close.

Without looking, she knew he was kneeling beside her. Without opening her eyes, she knew he was going to kiss her. She thought she was ready. She thought she knew what to expect. The longing she'd been feeling since their first kiss, since she'd watched his strong back riding in front of her on his bike, suddenly hit her, full force. And the longing grew, the need to feel his lips on hers, his body pressed against hers, overwhelming her. With a shock, she realized how much she wanted—*needed*—his kiss. And then it happened.

Softly he kissed the corner of her mouth and then her ear. The sweep of his tongue against the sensitive lobe left her dazed and breathless. She wound her arms around his neck, her fingers tangled in his hair. She inhaled deeply, unable to get enough of the all-male scent of leather and Quincy. He shifted his body until he was lying on top of her, his hips pressed against hers, his chest against the achingly sensitive tips of her breasts.

"*This* is what I'm doing here," he whispered in her ear. "Now you know." It was as simple as that. Basic animal attraction that neither of them could deny. Instinctively, she knew that it was for one day and that was it. They would have—*she* would have—one day under the sun, hidden from the world by the tall grass and the soft, undulating hills.

Then his mouth covered hers with a possessiveness that shocked her with its fierceness, and her thoughts became scrambled, overloaded with sensation. He couldn't possess her. Nobody could. But he did. He parted her lips with his tongue and she moaned softly, moving her hands along the muscles of his back, wanting to be close, closer. Her breath caught in her throat and she trembled. She was not thinking rationally. She wasn't thinking at all. All she could do was feel, and what she felt was a wild recklessness. . . .

He pulled her onto her side to face him and she felt the scrape of his jaw against her cheek. Her arms tightened around him. His hands moved under her shirt and grazed the silk of her bra. She shuddered. Frantic with need, he unfastened it and held the fullness of her breasts in his hands, massaging the buds with his thumbs.

"Abby." The sound of his voice, full of wonder, rich with longing, sent tremors shooting through her body. The coarse grass pressed into her bare skin where he'd pulled her shirt up, and a sandpiper cried overhead, seeming to take her feelings and voice them where she could not.

Quincy tenderly kissed her, then braced himself on one arm and looked at her. His breath was caught somewhere between his ribs. Abby lay on her side looking at him, wide-eyed, expectant. His heart went into overdrive—she was so beautiful. Instinctively he knew that it was now or never for them. They'd never be alone again, not like this, far from prying eyes and well-intentioned matchmakers. And he wanted her more than he'd ever wanted anything. Except the ranch. He ran his hand around the curve of her cheek and stopped at her chin. As much as he wanted Abby, he wanted the ranch more. Besides, he couldn't have her unless he told her who he was and what he wanted. And he wasn't going to do that. Not now, not ever.

He pressed his lips together and tried to smile. "Sorry about that," he said. "It must have been the wine."

She sat up abruptly and tugged at her shirt, her eyes blinking back tears. "And nothing to do with me." The look in her eyes sent a shaft of pain through his chest.

"It had everything to do with you," he corrected hoarsely, kicking himself for hurting her *and* for caring that he'd done so. "But you're my boss and I'm not somebody you want to get involved with."

"Why don't you let me decide that?" she asked, standing and fastening her bra with her back to him.

"Because." He looked up at her and swallowed, feeling like a complete sleaze. "You don't have all the facts."

She whirled around. "Do you?" There were tears glistening in her eyes, but even he could tell that they were tears of frustration and anger, not sadness. His spirits sank even lower. He wouldn't mind if she hated him, he deserved it, but he couldn't stand it that he'd hurt her. Suddenly he wished that the whole thing were over, the failure of the ranch and his taking it over, everything.

Then she'd find somewhere else to go and someone else to…to care about. Why, with her looks and her bottled-up passion, she was ripe for someone. He just wished it was him. The idea of someone else taking her off for a picnic in the tall grass made him feel sick. The idea of someone else marrying her and taking her to bed, made his heart grow cold with despair in the hot sun.

Numbed with suppressing the truth and his feelings for so long he silently watched her pack the remains of the lunch. With stiff, rigid movements, she piled the plates and containers into her backpack. He got to his feet and his knees buckled. Catching himself, he quickly glanced at Abby, but she hadn't noticed. He felt like he'd been punched in the gut. He deserved to be. She didn't deserve to be treated the way he'd just treated her. Hell, he'd lied to her from the beginning, led her on. She deserved better and if it was the last thing he did, he'd make sure she got it. Even if that meant never touching her again. He tried to breathe deeply, but there was something caught at the back of his throat. He guessed that something was guilt or remorse. Whatever it was called, it felt awful.

He wanted to take her back in his arms, run his hands up her back, along her shoulders, tell her he'd leave and get out of her life. But he couldn't tell her that, he thought, squaring his jaw. This was *his* ranch. It always had been, always would be. Right now she was probably wishing she'd never met him, never invited him back to the house and never hired him, but that wasn't his fault.

She was too generous, too kind, too trusting. She was also stubborn, willful and determined. He could see that it wasn't going to be easy to talk her into leaving the ranch. But, damn, if he didn't wish she wouldn't look like that— like he'd pulled the rug out from under her. How would she look when he pulled the whole ranch out from under her?

They bicycled down the hill, bumping over ruts, crashing around corners, never stopping, never looking back. It was the only way to go. It took a certain recklessness, a willingness to point the bike in the right direction and let go. She had what it took and so did he. Hands clamped around rubber handle grips, eyes straight ahead into the sun, they rode single file. He didn't look back to see if she was behind him. He could feel her presence as surely as he felt the sun in his face and the wind in his hair. He knew where she was and exactly how she looked. He'd memorized her face, every freckle, every tiny line in her forehead, her smile...and her tears.

Pulling up in front of the house, they found Mountain Mike sitting in his van waiting for them. A few guests had returned, most were still out. They returned the bikes and noticed Pop leaning against the old maple in the front yard, chewing on a stem of grass. He tilted the brim of his old worn Stetson back and gave them a smug smile.

"Where y'all been?" he asked, his eyes traveling hopefully from Quincy to Abby and back again.

"Out," Abby said tersely, and Pop's smile faded.

"For a ride," Quincy explained, slanting a glance at Abby. She gave him a look that chilled and rebuked at the same time.

"Didn't know ya could ride," Pop said to Quincy.

"Yep." Quincy wondered how long the nightmare would continue. How long would he have to stand there and make conversation knowing Abby never wanted to see him again? She edged around him, her eyes on the front door of the house, but Pop was too quick for her.

"Where'd ya go?" he asked, blocking her way.

"To the pond."

"Do any fishin'?" Pop asked.

"Just a picnic," Abby explained, her voice as taut as a violin string.

"That's all?" Pop's voice rose.

"That's all," Quincy said firmly, and watched Abby escape up the front steps.

Pop gave Quincy a look that made him feel like sinking into a hole somewhere. The look clearly said, *What have you done now? I told you not to hurt her and anyone can see she's hurting bad.*

Quincy had no answer for Pop. He knew what had happened and he wasn't proud of what he'd done. He'd almost blown it. Almost lost his cover... and his heart, too.

Chapter Eight

That night the fates finally smiled at Quincy's hopes of discouraging Abby's guests. After tossing and turning for hours, trying to think of ways of getting rid of her subtly, a bat came flying in his window, skillfully maneuvering in the total darkness. Without thinking twice, Quincy was on his feet and stumbling across the floor of the small bedroom in pursuit of the animal. Quincy, despite his fear of spiders, wasn't afraid of bats. In fact, he appreciated their ability as mammals who could fly.

Quickly pulling his jeans on over his shorts, he managed to grab the small warm body of the brown bat as it circled the room. Holding the poor critter gently with one hand, he stepped quietly into the dark night and headed for the bunkhouse. Though unafraid of bats himself, he was counting on the fact that many people dreaded them and had weird beliefs about the furry flying things. It was his feeling that this was only because they flew at night and were seldom seen up close. At the moment he actually didn't care *why* most people felt the way they did, he just hoped that a bat flying in a bunkhouse in the night would not be the most welcome sight in the world. Because if guests kept having a wonderful time, it would encourage more guests to come. And if the cows continued to produce more cows the way they were, there was no way this ranch was going to fail anytime soon. It was the last thing he wanted.

However, this state of affairs left him in an uncomfortable position. On the one hand, he was proud of the work they were doing—Pop, the boys, Abby and himself. On the other, it was his opinion that they could be doing so much better if they didn't have to worry about guests and could just concentrate on the cattle. Sure, he could see the guests appreciated the ranch, but there were other guest ranches. They didn't have to come here.

He had to admit it, though. He admired Abby's hard work. He admired a lot more about her, too, so much so, that he found himself tormented by second thoughts even now, as he walked softly down the path with the soft, warm body of the little bat in his hands. It was getting so he looked for Abby's smile, worried when she was worried, and tried to help when things went wrong. Which meant he was forgetting his larger goals. Forgetting the *real* reason he was there. Forgetting the harsh lesson he'd learned too well— that women could turn your world upside down when you least expected it, when you trusted them.

He knew he'd hurt her up there at the pond with what she perceived as a rejection, but what he knew was just self-protection. He hadn't even gone in to dinner. He couldn't face her knowing what she must think of him. And tonight he'd lain in bed for hours, listening to her footsteps overhead, thinking about the sunlight on the pond, the color of her eyes, the wind in her hair and the smooth touch of her skin.

As he walked through the dark he decided to think of this as an experiment. If people were afraid of bats, he comforted himself, then they shouldn't be on a ranch to begin with. Relaxing a little, he took note that there was a ladder propped against the bunkhouse, left behind from some roof repair done earlier. He tested it by climbing up the first few rungs. It wobbled, but he continued to climb until he reached the second-floor window. The window to the women's dorm. It was meant to be. Somehow he knew that women and bats wouldn't mix.

He was right. He let the quivering bat go through the open window and almost before he hit the bottom rung of the ladder he heard the screams, the pandemonium. He rounded the corner of the bunkhouse and almost ran into Abby, her thick terry-cloth robe wrapped tightly around her waist, her eyelids heavy with sleep. Instinctively he reached for her arm and held on to her.

"What's wrong?" she asked.

"I don't know. I just got here myself." Funny how easily the lie slipped off his tongue. The more he did it, the easier it got. He wasn't quite sure that was a blessing, though.

Her eyes were wide with concern and she pulled her arm away and hurried to the front door of the bunkhouse. The guests had run into the lecture room in various stages of dress, everything from shirts to pajamas. He didn't recognize them without their spandex shorts.

Abby was mobbed, everyone speaking at once until they finally got the message across. There was a bat loose upstairs and they were terrified. Some thought it was rabid, while others were convinced it was a vampire bat, come to suck their blood. Abby's gaze searched for Quincy's over the heads of the guests, her gaze imploring him to do something.

He nodded and walked up the stairs, finding the bat expertly circling the dark hallway. After several fruitless lunges, he captured it for the second time that night and brought it down the stairs with him. More screams, more terror, just to see it up close. Some guests huddled in the corner, others approached timidly with curiosity.

Taking a deep breath, he looked around himself at the guests. This was his chance, his opportunity to describe bats with rabies, and expand on the topic of vampire bats who lived on the blood of other animals and humans, with an aside about the dangers of flying foxes, of course. But before he could say anything, Abby stepped forward and told the crowd it was a harmless brown bat. Without missing a beat, she then went on and talked about its keen sense of hearing that allowed it to fly in the dark by using a rare system of radar. Not only was it harmless, she said in a firm, quiet voice, but it performed a valuable service by eating harmful insects.

As Quincy stood, holding the bat in his hands, floored by her unflappable approach to it all, the guests came up to him to gaze into the mammal's blinking eyes. Slowly they came to see the skin stretched over its tail that allowed it to fly. One woman reached out to touch its tiny head. He let someone else hold it for a minute. Then he decided that both he and the bat had had enough excitement for one night. He opened the front door and let it go. And without a word he went, too, back to the house, back to his room, where he closed the door firmly behind him.

He lay flat on his back, staring at the ceiling, still wearing his jeans, no shirt, no shoes, no socks, cursing his blown opportunity, his lack of willpower. He'd let Abby take over, turning the situation into a learning experience instead of a frightening one. If he had just seized the initiative, he could have had them on the next plane out of there.

But just one look into Abby's eyes and he'd gone up and captured it for her. He'd turned into Ranger Rick, protector of lost animals. Standing there, while she gave her speech when he should have let it loose again, he'd totally ruined everything. What was wrong with him? he wondered with disgust. He heard footsteps on the kitchen floor, steps that paused at his closed door. Abby's footsteps. He held his breath.

He couldn't take any more temptation. Not today. He willed her to keep walking, to go up the stairs…for her own sake and for his. If she thanked him again, he might just explode into a thousand pieces. When she finally passed by, he buried his face in his pillow to keep from calling her name. What was wrong with him? he asked himself again, desperation snaking through him.

Despite everything, he wanted her, so much he thought about stumbling up the stairs and following her into her room. Groaning, he gripped the edge of the mattress and didn't fall asleep until dawn.

Quincy avoided her for the rest of the week. She helped matters by avoiding him. Once he felt her eyes on him during dinner when she passed by with a basket of fresh dinner rolls, but when he looked up she looked away so fast he almost missed the look in her eyes, a combination of hurt and pride. He didn't know what to say to her even if he'd had the opportunity, so he didn't say anything.

When the cyclists left at the end of the week, he asked Pop who was coming next. Pop said he didn't know, he should ask Abby. Quincy didn't say he couldn't do that because he wasn't speaking to her and she wasn't speaking to him, so he simply watched and waited, but by Sunday noon nobody had come. The air was still and hot as the inside of an oven, the heat shimmering in the air, dust clogging the lungs of cows and men both.

He, Curly, Rocky and Pop were branding. The pens were filled with restless cattle and the air with the hot smoke from the branding irons. When it came to branding the bull, they cut the mark in its horn, but the branding itself was more out of tradition than fear of cattle rustling. It would take a very brave or very stupid man to try to rustle that bull away. It took all four of the men to etch a Z into its horn. They took the bull back to his fenced pen in the far pasture where he snorted and angrily tossed his head.

As they rode back to the barn under the blazing sun, Curly wiped the sweat from his brow and mentioned Abby had told him to take the week off.

Quincy's mouth fell open in amazement. "What about branding?"

"She says we can do it next week, when the families come. There aren't any guests this week."

"All the more reason we should get it done now," Quincy remarked flatly.

Curly and Rocky looked at Quincy uneasily.

"I don't know about you, but I'm goin' to see my cousin over to Cottonwood Falls," Pop said. "Like to get away today before the rain comes."

Quincy raised his eyes to the cloudless sky and shot him a surprised look.

"Feel it in my bones," Pop said. "Ya know the cattle will still be here next week. They ain't goin' no place. What about you?"

Quincy shook his head. "Haven't decided." So Abby had told them all to take the week off, but hadn't bothered to tell him. Maybe she thought he didn't deserve a break, since he'd just started working there. For nothing, too, he reminded himself. The others were getting paid.

"Can't do much brandin' in the rain, anyway," Pop concluded, looking at the sky again.

Quincy followed his gaze. The only thing he could see were some huge, heavy, white clouds far off on the horizon. But Pop always claimed his arthritis gave him a special insight into predicting weather.

"Whatever you say," Quincy said. "I'll hang around for a while. Maybe get some things done."

Pop and the boys left before dinner and despite his good intentions to get some things done, Quincy found himself wandering aimlessly from the barn to the corral to the henhouse and back again. The wind picked up and spun the weather vane on top of the barn so he couldn't tell where it was coming from. The white clouds in the distance were turning gray and he knew if Pop were there he'd say, "I told ya so."

He fed the cattle and horses and put them in the barn just in case it did rain. Then he went to the kitchen and stood just inside the door, wondering where Abby was, wondering if she, too, had taken the week off. She deserved it, but of course the ranch was her responsibility and she couldn't just leave. She needed to get away, though. The brief glimpses of her he'd had this past week had showed circles under her eyes and a certain strain around her mouth. Not that he'd been looking. Not much.

He sniffed the air. There was a rich, warm smell of tomato sauce and cheese coming from the oven. Why? There was no one here, but him. While he was standing there, his hip against the door, she came into the kitchen from the dining room and stopped abruptly the moment she saw him. Unable to control himself, his eyes hungrily traveled the length of her body, from her oldest, down-at-the-heels shoes up to her bare legs, past her shorts and to the oversized shirt knotted at her waist. Finally his gaze met hers and stopped. Her eyes were wide and vulnerable, and something within him did an odd flip. Darned if the woman didn't get to him.

"Everyone's gone," he said hoarsely.

"I know."

"I thought maybe you'd taken off, too," he said, clearing his throat casually.

"Me? Who'd feed the chickens and cows and horses?"

"I could manage. You, however, need a break."

"So do you," she countered, her eyes darkening slightly.

"What happened? I thought this was City Slicker Week."

She took an apron from the hook on the wall and tied it around her waist, seeming to take an inordinate amount of time to adjust it just so. "It was, but they canceled. I meant to tell you, but . . ." She bent over to look in the oven.

"That's all right. I don't have any place else to go."

"Neither do I," she said, straightening and meeting his gaze. The knowledge that this place was home to the both of them slowly sank into Abby's overloaded conscious. Inwardly, she gathered her composure. She would not let herself feel responsible for Quincy. He was quite capable of taking care of himself. She didn't have to cook for him. In fact, she'd only made the extra portions of lasagna to have something to do. Without guests and the boys, she felt at loose ends, she hadn't realized how much she needed to be needed.

"Why'd they cancel?" he asked, hanging his hat on the rack inside the door. He hoped she didn't notice the slight shaking in his hands. God, it had been so long since they'd been alone. "Did they hear about the bat?"

She smiled and a strange warmth flooded his chest, as if he'd suddenly come in from the cold. He hadn't realized how much he'd missed her smile, how it lighted the room, how it made him feel inside. Damn.

"I think the bat was a plus," she said.

"Thanks to your lecture," he added. "Where'd you learn about bats, at the Lazy Susan?"

"I don't know," she confessed. "Just some useless information I picked up somewhere that got stuck in a corner of my mind."

"It came in handy," he said, then could've cut out his tongue. Where had that note of pride come from? he wondered with disgust. What was he trying to do, sabotage himself?

The wind picked up and rattled the window behind him. Startled, he turned and frowned at the gathering storm clouds in the distance.

She crossed the kitchen and stood next to him, holding the curtain to one side. "What's going on out there?" she asked.

"Pop predicted rain. Looks like he's right, as usual." He opened the back door and stepped outside. Abby followed him. Together they stared off into the distance, where the dark clouds blocked the last of the sunset. "Thunderheads," Quincy explained, pointing to the horizon. As if on cue, a roll of thunder rumbled across the sky and a scattering of raindrops blew across the fields. "Turn on the radio," he told her. "Get the weather report. I'm going to check on the horses." A jagged shard of light lit the sky, followed by a roar of thunder.

Before she could protest, he'd gone running across the field to the barn. Abby went into the parlor to turn on the radio. Tornado spotters were describing cumulonimbus clouds over Emporia, heading for Tornado Alley. Even without knowing what a cumulonimbus cloud was, or where Tornado Alley was, she was filled with a gnawing dread in the pit of her stomach. Visions of flattened houses and barns tossed in the air filled her mind.

Abby went back to the kitchen and then stepped outside, her eyes straining to catch a glimpse of Quincy. As far as she could see, the tall grass was bending in waves ahead of the coming storm, and the wind began to howl, blowing her back against the house. She gripped the doorknob behind her and out of the darkness Quincy appeared tall and strong. He grabbed her by the arm and pulled her back into the kitchen.

"What'd they say?" he asked. The burst of rain that had caught him had plastered his hair to his head, and his shirt stuck to his chest.

"Tornado warning," she gasped.

His grip on her arm tightened. "Let's get down to the storm cellar."

Turning off the oven, he let her go get a flashlight, then they went back out the door. The door slammed behind them and they edged their way around the house, the growing force of the wind a foe that battled them every inch, threatening to push them back at every step. Abby, frightened by the sudden fierce atmosphere around them, clung to Quincy with her arms around his waist. She followed him, allowing him to block the wind, lead the way. The roar of the wind was deafening, terrifying. She stumbled on a branch that had blown in their path. Quincy reached behind him to wrap his arms around her. She dug her face into his back, tears mingling with rain.

She knew that barns and houses weren't the only things that were blown away. People were picked up and tossed into the next county, too. If she had to be tossed somewhere, though, she hoped she'd be tossed with Quincy, because he'd know what to do. He'd been through these before. And if she had to be stuck in a storm cellar with anyone, she'd rather be stuck with Quincy. If they ever got there, that is. It seemed to her they'd circled the house several times by now and had never come to the big, wide, flat doors, angled off from the siding, that led to the cellar.

Finally Quincy stopped and she loosened her grip around his chest. He reached down, pulled on the handle of a storm door and held the door up while pushing her down the steps ahead of him. She turned and held out her hand. He grabbed it and jumped down the steps before the door banged shut over their heads.

By the light of her flashlight, she checked out the room. She'd had little cause to be in it all that often since she'd bought the ranch. Now she carefully took it all in. It was small, with a chair in one corner and a wooden crate in the other. There was an old trunk shoved against the wall. Shelves lined the other wall and held jugs of water, a first-aid kit and a kerosene lamp. It was damp and musty, but the sound of the storm was now only a dull roar. All of a sudden she became aware of herself. Her shirt was wet and clinging to her skin and her rain-soaked hair dripped onto her forehead and down the back of her neck.

"There should be dry clothes and blankets in that trunk," Quincy said as he walked over and poured kerosene into the lamp.

Abby's eyebrows puckered, but she moved over and raised the lid of the trunk and looked inside. Sure enough, there was a stack of neatly folded shirts, pants, an old slicker and two wool blankets.

"How did you know?" she asked, confusion sweeping over her. Was there anything the man didn't know?

Quincy silently got a match from the box on the shelf and struck it. The match sputtered and he held it to the lamp's wick. It caught the flame and filled the room with a warm, yellow light. He shrugged as casually as he could. Real smart, McLoud. "I've been in storm cellars before. They're all pretty much the same."

"How often?" she asked.

"Uh, once or twice every season."

"And you always lived through it," she remarked. Any suspicion or doubt because of his familiarity were gone, her eyes wandering involuntarily to the heavy doors that kept out the wind and the rain.

"So far," he said with a reassuring grin.

"What about..." She hesitated, a sinking feeling in the pit of her stomach. "The rest of the ranch, the buildings, the animals?"

"We just hope for the best. Tornadoes are notoriously fickle."

"Did you ever lose anything?"

"Yep," he said. "A few head of cattle once. A couple of outbuildings another time. Better get out of those wet clothes. We may be here awhile."

"What about you?" she said, watching the water drip from his hair down the side of his face.

"After you," he insisted.

She looked around the tiny room. If she was going to change, it was going to have to be right here. And this didn't seem the time or the place to be modest. She sifted through the clothes in the trunk and brought up an old pair of bib overalls and a sweatshirt with Kansas State Aggies in large letters across the front.

Quincy sat on the wooden crate in the corner and picked up a very old copy of *National Geographic* and seemed to study it with great interest. Cautiously, she let her jean-shorts fall to the ground and then quickly pulled up the bibs, bringing them up to her chin before removing her wet shirt over her head. The sweatshirt felt warm and soft against her damp skin. It smelled faintly of mothballs and something else that was pungent and oddly familiar. A pair of wool socks completed her change.

"Your turn," she said, wincing at the brightness in her tone. Lord, you'd think she'd never changed with a man in the room.

He looked up and stared at the letters on the sweatshirt for a long time. Heat suffused her and she shifted self-consciously, crossing her arms under her breasts.

"What's wrong?" she asked uncomfortably.

"Looks like something I used to wear."

"You went to Kansas State? What a coincidence."

"Not really. Half of Kansas went to KSU, the other to the university."

"It feels good," she said impulsively, then could have kicked herself.

His eyes darkened to the color of the stormy sky outside. "Looks good, too."

She blushed. "Go ahead. Get changed. I promise not to look." She grabbed the magazine he'd been reading and buried her head in it. Inside, she could feel herself burning up, and it wasn't from embarrassment. She'd promised not to look, but she hadn't promised not to think about how he looked stripped down to his shorts, his skin covered with a damp sheen from his wet clothes. With a start, she stopped her wandering thoughts. He'd proven how much command he had over his emotions, now she would do the same. No matter how fast her heart beat, how much tension throbbed in the air between them, she would keep her cool today.

Even if they had to stay in this little room for days, she would never admit how close she'd come to making love to him by the pond. With an inward groan, she realized that maybe she didn't have to. Maybe he already knew. Probably he did. That was why he'd been avoiding her all week. How embarrassing to have a woman throw herself at you when you weren't interested in her.

It was better this way, she thought, settling into the chair in the corner and turning the pages without seeing what was on them. Much better. He'd drawn the lines and now they both knew where they stood. She was the employer, he was her employee. Despite that, he often gave the orders. The trouble was, he was always right. Today, however, she hadn't minded following his orders. She owed him her safety. And so much else. She tried to picture herself alone in the house or alone in the shelter. She was glad she wasn't alone. She was glad he was here.

She looked up from her magazine just as he was buttoning an old flannel shirt over his broad chest. She watched as his lean fingers moved down the opening of the shirt. A flashing image of how they'd felt on her skin came to her.

They'd been warm and slightly rough, yet gentle, as he'd
moved his hands all over her body. Her mouth went dry.

"I—I'm glad you stayed around, Quincy. I must admit I
was scared out there."

He nodded. "Me, too."

The magazine slid out of her hands and landed on the ce-
ment floor. "You, scared?"

He looked around at the limestone walls, anything so he
wouldn't have to look at her, huddled and adorable in his
old sweatshirt. "I'm scared of tornadoes, spiders and
women." He closed the lid of the trunk. "But not in that
order."

She rested her elbows on her knees. "*All* women?"

He propped his foot on the crate in the corner and stared
at the toe of his boot. He tried to ignore the fact he was
about to talk about things he'd never admitted to anyone
else. This woman had the oddest effect on him. "Not all
women," he said without looking up. "What really scares
me is how I could have made such a big mistake as to get
married in the first place. My ex-wife didn't belong on a
ranch, I did. I was happy, I didn't realize she wasn't. Even
when I was at home, I wasn't really at home. I was out on
the range with the boys and the cattle."

She held perfectly still, hoping he'd continue. When he
talked, she didn't hear the wind or the rain outside, didn't
think about the funnel-shaped cloud that could be headed
their way. Besides, she was curious about Quincy's life, and
his opening up was rare. She didn't want to miss any of it.
"She divorced you for that?" she asked.

"Well, then I joined the reserves. I thought she'd be glad,
glad of the extra money if not glad to have me serve my
country. She *was* glad…to have me gone. She had a chance
to find someone else. And that's the way it ended."

Abby's eyes widened at the flat, unemotional delivery of
what must have been a painful experience for him. "Just
like that?"

"Just like that. I got a letter from her while I was in the
Gulf. And I never saw her again."

"Do you miss her?" Abby asked, leaning forward on the edge of the chair.

"Do you miss your husband?" he countered.

"I don't miss him criticizing me. Telling me what to do and how to do it. I don't miss feeling like a failure all the time, but . . ."

She felt his eyes on her face, his quiet intensity, waiting for her to continue.

She pushed a damp strand of hair from her forehead. "I don't know, sometimes I miss having . . . someone to share things with. Day to day. That's why I love having guests all the time. That's why I've been feeling a little low today knowing no one was coming, knowing the boys were taking off. I thought you'd be gone, too."

He shook his head, his eyes never leaving her face.

"That's right, you have no place to go. I'm sorry about that."

"I'm not. I like it here." He looked around at the bare walls, at the low ceiling. "No spiders."

"What about me?" she asked. "You're not afraid of me, are you?"

He gave her a long look, so intense that she wished she hadn't asked. The silence stretched out as he pondered his answer and her heart pounded faster and faster. His gaze heated the air between them. She was afraid he'd say yes, more afraid he'd say no. She cleared her throat.

"Anyway," she said, "you shouldn't be afraid of women. They like you."

He laughed out loud and broke the tension between them. "How do you figure?"

"When I was in town, I heard some things."

"I heard some things about you, too," he said.

She blushed furiously. "I'll bet."

"Good things. Men like *you*."

Her blush deepened and she stood up restlessly, fanning her face with her hand. They were getting into dangerous territory and there was no escape. It was one thing to discuss men and women in general, but when it came down to getting personal, it made her uncomfortable. The truth was, she didn't care very much what men thought about her. It was Quincy whose opinion mattered.

"We should have brought your lasagna," he suggested.

"It'll be there when we get back." She sobered. "Unless it's blown away with the kitchen. Do you think that's possible?"

"Anything's possible in a tornado. School buses picked up and set back down again right side up. You have insurance, don't you?"

"Yes, of course. But I could never replace my calves, my house..." Her eyes filled with tears, thinking of her ranch being destroyed by a black cloud. Of coming up out of the cellar to find it flattened, everything gone, the barn, the horses....

"You really do love it, don't you?" he asked, his voice oddly fierce.

"Yes, but I'm not even going to think the worst. How long will this last?" she asked, pacing restlessly.

He stood and stretched.

"Not long. An hour maybe. When the rain hits the ground the way it was doing out there it cools the earth and pretty soon there isn't enough heat energy to make the air rise. Don't worry, you won't be stuck here much longer with me. The storm can't last without that air rising, and tornadoes depend on the thunderstorms that caused them in the first place."

"How do you know all that?"

"Everybody in Kansas knows that. They don't call it Tornado Alley for nothing. Did you feel the tension in the air just before the storm? All that pent-up energy, all that potential for sudden change?"

"I felt it," she admitted, "but I thought it was me."

He gave her a long, searching look, his eyes as dark as thunderclouds.

"About the other day," she continued. "You were right to put a stop to it when you did." There, she'd said it. Gotten it off her chest at last.

"I don't know about that." He stood up, his head almost grazing the plaster ceiling.

"One of us had to, I'm afraid it wasn't about to be me." She buried her face in her hands, unable to look him in the eye, remembering how eager she'd been, almost begging him to make love to her. The humiliation threatened to engulf her.

Quincy couldn't stand it. He kneeled down in front of her and gently pried her fingers from her face. "Don't," he said, holding her hands tightly in his. "Whatever happened there was my fault. Whatever didn't happen was my fault, too. I've thought about it, regretted it ever since, but..."

"But I'm not right for you, am I?" she asked, staring into his eyes, feeling his pulse beat in time to hers.

"That's not it at all. It's me. *I'm* not right for *you*. I'm not right for anybody."

"Why not?" she asked. She was having a harder and harder time at finding any of his faults. She'd come to know him, realize that his gruff, take-charge manner was just that, a facade, and that underneath he was thoughtful, considerate, tough, strong and sexy, too. Maybe he wasn't right for her, but just because he'd been divorced once didn't mean he wouldn't be right for somebody else. Although the idea of him being somebody else's husband made her feel sick with anxiety. It was hard to think he wouldn't always be there with her on her ranch. But, of course, he had to leave one of these days. Maybe soon. She looked at him, waiting for an answer to her question.

"'Why not?'" he repeated. "Trust me, I'm not going to settle down again with anyone."

"That's the funny thing," she said, "I do trust you."

He opened her hand then, and ran his fingers along the life line of her palm, tracing the rounded contours with his thumb until she felt the same breathless energy surge through her that caused the tornadoes of Kansas.

Quincy saw her breasts rise and fall under the thick sweatshirt. He knew he should turn away, pull his hands from hers, but the room was so small and the scent of her hair and her skin had invaded his senses and shut off the current to his brain. If he'd had any sense at all, the word "trust" would have sent warning bells ringing all over the place. But he couldn't think. All he could do was try to keep the fires of passion under control. Slowly he untangled his fingers from hers and cupped her face in his hands, forcing her to meet his gaze.

"Abby," he said, his voice catching.

She leaned forward, so close their lips were almost touching, so close her face blurred in front of his eyes. Just one touch, one taste, he promised himself, and then the storm would be over. Not the storm outside, but the one that raged inside him. What to do about her, what to do with her, or without her, was something to worry over later. He pulled her toward him, angling her face with his hands so he could mold his lips to hers. One kiss before they rejoined the world outside, he promised himself. Before he went back on the straight and narrow and kept those promises he'd made to himself.

But as his lips joined hers, he knew this wasn't just any kiss. It was a drug, an intoxicant that turned his blood to molten lava. There was no way he could stop after just one, any more than he could have stopped the tornado from its course. It was fate. It was destiny. And until the storm inside himself wore itself out, he was powerless to stop kissing her.

She was down on her knees now, her thighs pressed against his, returning his kisses with reckless abandon, her hands gripping his shoulders, her breath coming fast and furiously, forgetting the past, ignoring the future, conscious only of the here and now. She heard the thunder, but knew it was only her heart pounding. Quincy filled her mind, her heart, her very being.

The taste of him sent waves of desire rushing through her body. A deep-seated need began somewhere deep inside her and throbbed its way to the surface. She clung to him for support. Her hands gripped his waist and then moved lower to shape his hips and then lower still until he moaned and she caught her breath in a sob.

She hated her clothes, hated his, too. She wanted to feel his skin next to hers, the heat of his body infusing hers. She wanted to erase the distance between them, wanted to be one with him, to feel whole again.

As if he knew that, he lifted the sweatshirt over her head and tossed it on the floor. He slid the straps of her overalls off her shoulders and unclasped her bra, removing it. The heat flooded her body and made her skin feel feverish. Her hair fell across her shoulders, brushed his face. She'd never felt this way before, so free, so deliciously wanton. The ache in the deepest, most sensitive part of her became a throbbing agony, begging for release even as his hands cupped her breasts.

He trailed hot kisses down her throat, and buried his face in the valley between her full breasts. She was so beautiful, more beautiful than he imagined. He raised his head and saw the answer to his unspoken question. She wanted him as much as he wanted her. The knowledge hit him with the force of a twister. A twister that was raging out of control right here in the cellar.

He couldn't get the buttons on his shirt unbuttoned. He ripped them off, just barely conscious of the banging, the pounding, inside his head. Until he realized it wasn't in his head at all, it was outside the cellar, and with the pounding a voice shouting his name.

Abby stared at him, her eyes dilated, her mouth parted, lips swollen from the passion of his kisses. "Somebody's out there," she whispered, pressing her forehead against his.

He nodded slowly, reaching blindly for her sweatshirt while she hooked the straps of the overalls with trembling fingers and stuffed her forgotten bra into her pocket. He pulled her shirt over her head for her, brushing the soft swell of her breasts with his hands. Then he turned and raised the door, the muscles in his arms shaking from the effort and the shock. Abby was right behind him. He felt the heat from her body; the smell of her hair followed him everywhere.

It was Pop standing there, his battered old hat dripping water, his jacket plastered against his wiry body. "Everybody okay in there?" he asked, grabbing the handle of the storm door.

"Fine," Quincy growled. "Where'd you come from?"

"Couldn't go off and leave knowin' ya was in the path of the twister," he explained, his eyes traveling from Quincy to Abby. "It's gone now, spun itself out. Ya can come up now." Pop reached for Abby's hand and she came up the steps while Quincy extinguished the lamp in the cellar.

"Any damage?" she asked Pop.

"Dunno. Alls I know is that the buildin's are still standin'. Sure am relieved to find you two down here." He paused and gave Quincy a penetrating look. "Hope I didn't interrupt anythin'."

Quincy attempted a look that said, *Don't be ridiculous,* but he had a hard time meeting Pop's eyes. So hard, in fact, he found it easier to sidestep him and follow behind Abby to the barn while Pop trailed behind.

The animals were nervous and restless, but the barn was intact. The bunkhouse windows were broken and there was water damage to the carpets and walls. Abby was quiet as they surveyed the damage to the meeting room, the same room she'd shown him with such pride the first day he'd come back. Even with her insurance, it was going to be a setback. It would take a while before everything was back to normal. In the meantime, Quincy boarded up the windows for her. Then the three of them went to the kitchen and ate the lasagna.

At least, Pop and Quincy ate. Quincy watched Abby, who was sitting across the table from him, staring off in the distance as if she'd lost her best friend instead of a few windows.

"It could have been worse," he commented, putting his fork down. He had the feeling that she cared more about the ranch than anything or anyone. Including him. He might as well not have been there, for all she cared. Strange how that should bother him, him being the one person in the world who understood how she felt. He was the one other person who cared more about the ranch than anyone. Or used to. Seeing her sitting there, swallowed up in his old sweatshirt and old overalls, he had a fierce desire to gather her up in his arms and finish what they'd started down in the cellar. But the time had passed, the moment was gone, never to come again, and that left him feeling frustrated, tense . . . and unbearably sad.

She looked as if she didn't remember anything. And there was no way to remind her. Especially with Pop watching him with an eagle eye to make sure he wasn't leading her on. Why didn't Pop worry about *him?* Why didn't he have a talk with Abby about *Quincy's* feelings? With hollow bitterness, he gave up. Quincy shoved his chair back from the table, excused himself and went out to feed the animals.

Chapter Nine

Abby stood in the middle of the second-floor women's dormitory with the insurance adjuster. He took pictures with a Polaroid camera, wrote notes on a stenopad and told her he was sorry it had taken a full week before he could get around to her. But there was so much other damage, so much more serious damage. A barn roof blown off across town, a silo down in another county, mobile homes completely destroyed. Yes, she was one of the lucky ones.

Lucky. If she heard that again she'd scream. One week of lost income was enough to set her back thousands of dollars. One week of backbreaking work picking glass out of the carpet, scrubbing water stains from the walls. And now to find out she wouldn't receive her settlement for weeks yet. And she was supposed to feel lucky? The insurance man closed his briefcase and left her standing in the middle of the room, staring out the one window that was still intact.

Not only had she lost the group of families who'd been expected to come this week, but she'd lost the Friends of the Prairie group, too. Scheduled for next week, they had canceled. They were worried. How could she blame them? She was worried, too. Worried about the ranch, worried about money, worried about the future. She couldn't guarantee there wouldn't be another tornado. She could only vouch for the safety of the storm cellar. But it would be hard to fit a group of guests in there. It was scarcely big enough for two. Especially if those two couldn't keep their hands off each other.

That week, in between cleaning up the mess and worrying, she had replayed the scene in the cellar over and over in her mind. What would have happened if Pop hadn't come back for them? Would they ever have come out? Would they have stayed there until they'd been consumed with passion, until the very storm itself had come and gone and they were lying on the floor in each other's arms, the force of their passion spent like the spinning funnel cloud that had destroyed everything in its path?

That was what passion did, she reminded herself harshly. It destroyed everything you wanted, everything you worked for. And she couldn't let anything or anyone come between her and her ranch. From now on, she was going to concentrate as never before on catching up to where she was before the storm. She'd had two close calls with Quincy. One at the pond and the other in the cellar. And that was enough. She couldn't afford to let it happen again.

She'd seen Quincy watching her this past week and she hoped by now he'd gotten the message. She was sorry she'd encouraged him, but she had no intention of continuing this crazy infatuation that gripped her. He must be confused by the mixed signals she was sending, so she wasn't going to send any more. If only he wouldn't look at her like that. Like there was unfinished business between them. Like he was waiting for her to say something. What *could* she say? She was sorry she'd behaved like a depraved farmer's daughter instead of the dignified owner of a cattle ranch? Sorry she found him so irresistible she couldn't keep her hands off him? The worst part was, she was only sorry they'd been interrupted. And that part she would never admit to anyone.

He fed the animals, took them out to pasture, gave orders to the boys, repaired fences, rode the range all with a calm competence. And she wondered how she had ever gotten along without him and how she'd get along when he left. Yes, things ran smoothly with him around. But after the Friends of the Prairie canceled, the Sunday School Teachers group withdrew for the week after that.

Abby sat in her parlor at the rolltop desk on Sunday, surrounded by unpaid bills and unused brochures. She couldn't blame people for being nervous. She couldn't blame the families who'd booked with her for going to Wisconsin instead. She couldn't even blame the Friends of the Prairie for staying in Nebraska. Until tornado season was over, people would be jittery. The only good thing was that the check from the insurance company had come and she'd had the bunkhouse windows repaired. But what good did it do if there were no guests to look out the windows and no one to walk on the fresh carpets?

She buried her head in her hands and didn't look up until she heard the front door open. Quincy stood just inside the door, allowing the fresh air to waft into the dark-paneled room. His jeans were dusty, his faded shirt wrinkled. Hatless, his strong features wore a cautious expression, as if he didn't know what or who he'd find there. Strange, she hadn't realized how stuffy and dark it was in there, until he came in.

As his eyes got accustomed to the cool darkness of the formal parlor, he saw Abby seated at her desk under a tasseled Tiffany lampshade, her hair the color of gold ingot under the lamplight.

"Come in," she called, her lips twisting in an effort to smile.

He walked across the faded carpet to the desk. He hadn't been this close to her since they'd left the storm cellar. She'd changed. Her blue eyes had lost their sparkle, her shoulders were slumped forward over her desk. Her fingers played restlessly with the stack of bills in front of her. She looked over his shoulder. Anywhere but at him.

"What's wrong?" he asked, bracing his hands against the edge of the desk.

"Nothing. Nothing that a new batch of guests wouldn't cure and a giant infusion of money."

"I can't bring back the guests," he said, guiltily thinking of how hard he'd tried to discourage them from coming. Now that they'd stopped, he didn't feel the great burst of joy he'd expected.

"No one can," she said. "Not after what happened. It will take some time before people forget that there was a lot of damage in this part of the state. Even though no one was killed and we came out okay, they're still scared. They saw the pictures in the papers of the destruction and they can't forget it."

"I guess everybody's got memories of the storm they can't forget," he said pointedly.

She looked up and her blue eyes blazed for a brief second, and he knew she'd understood exactly what he meant. Why wouldn't she admit it? Why was she trying to pretend it had never happened? It wasn't that he didn't feel guilty about having taken advantage of the situation. He just wanted to know if it had meant anything to her, if it had been more than just an explosion of pent-up desire. Hell. She was certainly more than just an object of desire to him. How much more, he didn't want to think about. Talk about being scared. Every time he looked at her, his heart pounded in his chest. This time he was scared of his feelings. So scared he was trying to bury them. But that didn't mean he appreciated her pretending nothing had happened between them.

"I can't bring back the guests," he repeated, "but I can loan you the money you need to pay your bills." His eyes swept over the paper on her desk. He couldn't believe his own words, but dammit, if it would bring her out of her funk, then he'd do it gladly.

"Thanks," she said, snapping her pen open and closed several times, "but I couldn't let you do that."

"Why not? I'd expect to be paid back when you're back on your feet again."

"When will that be?" she asked somberly, self-deprecation in her tone.

"I can't believe I'm hearing you talk like this. Is this the woman who wouldn't let anything stand in her way?" he asked, sitting on the edge of her desk and leaning forward intently.

She tilted her chair back and looked at him. "That was *before* I got hit by a tornado."

"Tornadoes are a way of life here, you'd better get used to them."

"Maybe I should have bought a ranch in Nevada."

His jaw tightened. That was what he'd been hoping she would do—buy a ranch somewhere else. But that was before. Now he wasn't so sure. He couldn't imagine the Kansas tall grass without her in the middle of it. "There are storms in Nevada, too, and flash floods and hail and drought. Are you prepared for that?"

"Maybe I'm just not cut out for this life," she replied in a lifeless tone.

"What are you talking about?" he demanded. "I've seen you out there on your horse, in the heat and the dust, and in the rain and the wind. The guests will come back. You'll see. You can't give up. Not now." He rubbed his head. What was he saying? He who never wanted to see another guest poke his head over the corral and ask to have his picture taken next to a cow.

She nodded, but he could see she wasn't convinced. "In the meantime..."

"In the meantime, let me lend you the money you need."

She shook her head. "I can't. You've already done too much for me."

He froze. If she only knew what he had done, how much he'd hoped she'd fail... and now he was offering her the money to keep going. *He,* of all people, was trying to cheer her up, the guy who'd barely been putting in his time until this moment. Now that it was here, he felt nothing, only an all-encompassing empathy for her he'd never felt for anyone else. Because he knew how he'd feel in her position.

"If I were in your place..." he began.

She looked up, interest sparking in her eyes. "What would you do?"

"Whatever it took to keep the ranch. Borrow, beg, steal, lie, cheat..."

"And you're suggesting I do the same?"

"Not all of those things, just one. Borrow."

She sighed. "I was brought up not to spend my money until I had it. I already have a big mortgage on the ranch. I had to do that. But going further in debt is too painful." Her gaze strayed to the stack of bills on her desk. Curly and Rocky hadn't even been paid this month. If she borrowed just enough... No, she couldn't do that, not from Quincy. Not from anybody.

She met his earnest gray gaze. How could anybody be that nice and that good-looking? With his shirtsleeves rolled up above his elbows, a smudge of dirt on his chin, a layer of dust on his boots, he was the best-looking, most rugged man she'd ever seen, on or off a ranch, in or out of a movie. She felt herself weaken. She dropped her pen and it landed on the rug and she didn't notice.

"Why would you lend me the money? I might not be able to pay it back. I might have to sell the ranch..." Her voice caught and she pressed her lips together, just thinking the unthinkable upset her.

"Because I don't need it. It's just sitting there gathering interest."

"Why don't you buy yourself a ranch with it? I know you want one."

"I will. One day. When I'm ready. Until then..."

She gripped the edge of the desk. "I'm touched by your generosity, Quincy. I really am. I don't want you to think I'm not grateful. You've given me so much since you came here..." Her voice quavered and she stopped to pull herself under control. "Your time, your support, your help and..."

"Hold on," he said, his ears turning red, his voice gruff "Let's not get carried away here."

"I'm not," she assured him. "I've been wanting to tell you that for a long time. Only I was afraid you'd be too proud to accept my gratitude."

"I'll accept your gratitude if you'll accept my money."

A reluctant smile tugged at the corners of her mouth. If it were only that simple. But it wasn't. Accepting a loan from Quincy was admitting she couldn't make it on her own, and she wasn't ready to do that yet. She shook her head slowly and reached down to find her pen.

Quincy got off her desk and walked to the door. Damn stubborn female. He should have known how proud she was. Admiration for her determination to go it alone rose in him. He never should have offered. She'd rejected him. If he didn't do it to her, she did it to him. He paused in front of the door and spun the handle around in his hand. Then he turned to face her again.

"What about this, then. Let me buy half the ranch from you. We'll be partners. I'll do what I do and you do what you do."

"The way we do now," she said.

His heart swelled with hope. "Yes." He stared at her, waiting for her answer, holding his breath while the grandfather clock ticked loudly in the hall. How could she refuse this time? There was no charity in this offer, no offense to her pride. Just a business deal, pure and simple. Sure, she wouldn't like to part with half the ranch, but it was better than losing it all. Which was where she was headed. He decided to expand a little on his plan.

"Then when the guests cancel, we can work harder on cattle production, and if the cattle have problems, we'll step up the guest program," he said.

"I thought you didn't like the guests."

"Some of them aren't so bad."

"Like the little girl you taught to ride?"

"All right, so I'm a sucker for little kids who aren't afraid of big horses."

"So how would things be different?"

He came halfway across the room and stopped. He couldn't get too close or he'd get carried away and promise her the moon. And she didn't want the moon. She got suspicious whenever he offered something for nothing. He had to keep it simple and keep his distance from those magnetic blue eyes.

"They wouldn't," he assured her. "You'd go back to doing what you do best, and I'd do what I do, only I use some money to expand the herd and hire some help." His heart was beating fast now—as fast as he was talking—just thinking about having some control again, being able to do what he wanted to do and still have Abby around. What their relationship would be he hadn't had time to think about it. If they were business partners it would have to be hands-off, on the other hand....

She stood up and walked slowly around the desk, then leaned back against it. Her eyes were shining and her shoulders were straight again. "That was probably the nicest thing you could have done. And I know you're going to think I'm an idiot for saying no."

"No?" He rocked back on his heels. He had pictured tears of gratitude. He had even felt her arms around him in a burst of emotion. But he had never expected her to say *no*.

"I'm tempted. I really am," she said. "I think you'd make a great partner. I mean, we're almost partners now. But I can't, not after what I've been through. I can't let you have half of my ranch. It's the only thing I've ever had that was all mine. And if it goes down, then I'll go down with it. Alone. I have to take full responsibility for its success or its failure. That's the way it's got to be." The words were definite, but there was a slight tremor in her voice she couldn't control.

"Sure about that?" he asked.

He saw a faint twitch of the muscle in her temple. "Sure."

"Okay." He tried to keep his tone light, a half smile on his face. He turned and let himself out into the bright afternoon sunshine and walked to the barn, although later he couldn't remember how he got there. So it was over. She'd rejected his offers—all of them. And it was no good pretending there wasn't something personal in it. If she had liked him enough, if she had trusted him enough, she would have said yes.

But why should she trust him? He went through the motions of saddling his horse to ride out to the south pasture. She knew next to nothing about him, and what she did know wasn't true. As he rode, he realized he'd done everything he could. He'd done his best to sabotage the ranch so it would fall into his hands, and that hadn't worked. She'd turned his attempts into advantages for the guests, witness both the bucket brigade and the invasion of the bat incident.

Despite his efforts—and thanks to the tornado—she was on her knees now. But he took no pleasure in it. Soon she'd be in foreclosure and then he could have the whole thing, not just half. Why should he worry? Things were better than he could have imagined. So why wasn't he jumping for joy instead of staring off into the sunset feeling like he'd been run over by a tractor? It wasn't the thought of having the ranch to himself without Abby, was it?

No, it was just that he couldn't stand to stay here any longer and watch her fall and not be allowed to help. He couldn't stand to see the sparkle disappear permanently from her eyes, to see her shoulders cave in under the strain. She didn't deserve all that after what she'd been through. So instead of staying around and watching everything fall apart, he'd leave. Just as he'd promised. He'd drift away just as easily as he'd drifted there.

That night he drove to town to avoid seeing her or Pop at dinner. He walked up and down Main Street, looking in the windows, admiring new tractors in the showrooms, avoiding the glances of people he knew. He wanted to leave right away, but he couldn't. He had to say goodbye. He'd do it in the morning. After he'd psyched himself up for it.

Because before he said goodbye, he knew he'd have to tell her the truth. He would tell her who he was and why he'd come to work for nothing. She'd be surprised, sure, but maybe she'd understand why he'd done it, how much he loved the place. Maybe she would have done the same in his place. No, he stopped his thoughts there. She wouldn't have done the same. She never would have lied to him. She didn't have it in her. Just one look in those earnest blue eyes and you knew how honest she was.

She'd told him the whole story of her life, her failed marriage, her failure to get pregnant—everything. She'd *trusted* him. That was the worst part. He drove back to the ranch and walked around the barn from where he'd parked his truck to the house. In her bedroom he saw a dim light burning, but he kept walking, to the back door and into his room. For the last time.

Upstairs in her bedroom, Abby sat up in bed and thought about what Quincy had said. Was she wrong in turning down his offer to be her partner? *Was* she letting her pride stand between her and her ranch? On the one hand, his money would give her a chance, a second chance. But on the other, it wouldn't be the same. Quincy had his own ideas of how to run a ranch. She didn't always agree. There would have to be compromises...*just like in a marriage.* And Abby wasn't good at marriage. She wasn't good at trying to live up to other people's expectations. Quincy wasn't exactly other people, though. He understood her.

She stretched out on her bed, in her crisp, cotton nightgown, with her head hanging over the edge, brushing her hair. Maybe if she let the blood rush to her head it would be easier to think. But for every reason she had to accept his offer, she found she had another to reject it. Quincy might understand her, but she sure didn't understand him. If he had so much money, why did he want to invest it in her ranch? Why not buy one of his own? That was what *she* would do. Maybe he really loved this ranch more than any other and preferred to have half of it instead of all of something else?

He hadn't come to dinner. His truck was gone. Maybe he'd left. Maybe because she'd turned him down. Maybe she should have thought it over. She *was* thinking it over. But he didn't know that. And it didn't do any good. She was on the brink of financial failure. Without guests, she couldn't pay the bills. The sale of the cattle would help, but it would be too little, too late.

The guests were her reason for having a ranch in the first place, and if they didn't want to come, there was no point in having a ranch at all. But the guests would come back. They just needed time to forget the storms, get over their fear. Meanwhile she needed money so she could wait for them to come back. Her thoughts went around in ever-increasing circles. Straightening up, she went to the open window and pulled back the curtain.

There it was, stretched out before her in the pale moonlight. Her ranch. Her cattle ranch. This was a working cattle ranch first and foremost, no matter how important the guests were to her. That was what drew the guests. And Quincy was the man who made it work. Pop helped. So did Curly and Rocky. But it was Quincy who made things happen. No one else cared about the cattle and the land the way he did. And she'd turned him down. Told him she didn't want his money or him as a partner.

How had that made him feel? She hadn't thought about his feelings until now. She hadn't realized that she might have hurt him by rejecting his offer of help. She only hoped he hadn't gone for good. There was no sound, not a breath of air tonight. She closed the window.

She tiptoed down the stairs and went into the kitchen, the linoleum cool against her bare feet. There was a light shining under his door. She hadn't realized she was holding her breath until she let it out with a whoosh. He hadn't left, not yet. She raised her arm to knock on his door, then dropped it. She wanted to say that she'd changed her mind, that she couldn't do without him. But she couldn't. Not yet. She'd tell him in the morning.

She hurried back up the stairs before he came out and confronted her. Back in bed, she thought about what he'd said. He was right, as usual. She needed his help. Just admitting it to herself flooded her with relief. Yes, everybody needed help at one time or another. In the morning she'd tell him she accepted. They'd be partners. She smiled to herself in the dark. *Partners.* With Quincy. She liked the sound of it.

After a sleepless night, Quincy finally got out of bed at five and rode to the top of the ridge to look down on the ranch. The ranch he loved so much it made his throat hurt to think of never seeing it again. He memorized the lines of the hills that undulated in the distance, the waving grass with the sun breaking over the horizon. He wanted to leave right away, but before he left he had to tell Abby the truth. She deserved to know who he was and what he'd done so she wouldn't regret his departure for one minute. That he could guarantee, once she'd heard his story.

Then she could get on with her life. She would make a success of the place without him. She had what it took, the perseverance and the sheer strength of will. Sure the tornado had gotten her down, but it was just temporary. She'd bounce back. He'd tell her that, if she'd listen.

In the distance he saw a horse and rider leave the barn and he knew even from that distance that it was her. His heart pounded, knowing the moment of truth was finally at hand. She followed the same trail he'd taken, her blond hair blowing in the early morning wind, her face tilted toward him. He thought she was smiling, but he wasn't sure. She had no reason to smile at him.

He didn't move and neither did his horse. He felt like a statue, carved of stone, only no statue ever felt like he did, filled with apprehension and dread. Closer and closer she came, her cheeks tinged pink in the early morning light, her hair like spun gold, her eyes the color of the sky. And she *was* smiling as she approached and jumped off her horse.

"I found you," she said, winding the reins around her hand. "I was afraid you'd left."

"Not yet."

"I don't blame you for being disgusted with me." She stood next to his horse, looking up into his eyes, shading her own with her hand as if it were high noon instead of early morning. "But I came to tell you I changed my mind. If it's not too late." She beamed an irrepressible smile up at him, hope, joy and excitement mingled in her expression.

He stared down at her, unable to believe his ears. It was so ironic, he almost laughed out loud. He brought his leg to one side and slid off his horse. He gripped her shoulders with both hands and watched the smile on her face fade.

"What's wrong?" she asked anxiously. "Is the offer not... Did you change your mind?"

"The offer stands," he said gruffly. "But I don't think you'll want to have anything to do with me once you hear what I've got to say."

She drew her eyebrows together in a frown. Then she sank into the tall grass and hugged her knees to her chest without looking at him. What was he talking about? Looking into his serious gaze, her heart sank. Whatever it was, she had a feeling she wasn't going to like it. He sat next to her, stared off into space and took a deep breath.

"I'm not sure where to start," he said.

"At the beginning," she suggested, her chin on her knees.

"I grew up on a ranch," he said. "You knew that. And I learned to rope and ride and brand from my father, who learned from his father. I never knew any other kind of life or any other ranch. My mother was a housewife, but a partner in every sense of the word. And I knew without a doubt that was the kind of life I wanted for myself. When I grew up, I went off to college and studied ranch management and when I got married, I married a Kansas girl. Even though she'd never lived on a ranch, I thought she'd adapt. I was so dense, I thought she had adapted...until I went off to war and she...took off. But first she sold the ranch and sent me half the money."

Abby turned toward him, her frown deepening. "But how...?"

"It wasn't exactly legal, although she had power of attorney. And, yeah, I could have gone to court, but I was in a state of shock losing everything at once like that. I felt so stupid, so naive, it took me a long time to recover."

Abby nodded sympathetically and Quincy's stomach twisted into a knot. Her sympathy wasn't going to last much longer.

"But you *did* recover," she said, resting her hand on his arm. Her fingers burned like a branding iron and he had to pull away.

"Yes. I recovered, finally, by coming back to the ranch."

"*This* ranch? The Bar Z?" she asked incredulously.

"That's right. This was my ranch—my family's ranch for three generations."

"Why didn't you say so?" she demanded.

"I was going to, the first day I met you, but I realized right away you'd never sell it back to me. You said it was love at first sight and I believed you. I loved it, too. So I thought I'd wait."

"For what?"

He didn't speak. It was too painful. He'd vowed never to lie to her again and he didn't have to. She caught on.

"Oh, I see. You knew I'd fail even then. You were just waiting for it to happen." She dropped her head against her knees.

"I didn't see how you could make it by yourself," he admitted. "But that was then."

"That's now, too," she said, her voice flat, empty and discouraged. "You were right. I *can't* make it. You've been very patient, waiting for me to fail."

"Not patient enough," he said, bracing his hands against the ground. "I was worried you'd never give up, so I...sabotaged the pump and let it run dry."

She stared at him with disbelief. "You...you..." Her mouth was so dry she couldn't speak, couldn't swallow. The man she'd learned to trust, to admire, to...to... She'd thought she knew him, but she didn't know him at all. He was a stranger—a stranger who'd come to take away her ranch—and he was just as underhanded as the wife who'd taken it away from him and sold it to her.

"I don't believe you," she said, her voice a bare whisper.

"There's more."

She clamped her hands over her ears. "I don't want to hear it."

"You've got to hear it. So you'll know it wasn't your fault."

"Why, what else did you do?"

"I let the bat loose in the dorm, to scare the women, so they'd leave. I wanted to get rid of the guests and turn it back into a cattle ranch and just a cattle ranch."

Abby's mind returned to the night when she'd been awakened by the women's screams. She recalled how she'd run into Quincy outside the bunkhouse, how she'd wondered how he'd gotten there so fast. She thought of the terror on their faces.

"How could you?" she asked. Her lips were numb, scarcely able to form the words.

"I wanted the ranch back. More than anything. I didn't know how else to get it."

"But it didn't work. You must have been disappointed. They all stayed."

He gave her a grim smile. "I know. I miscalculated."

The image of the bat flying around in the dorm ricocheted around in her brain. A small sound escaped from the back of her throat. It was a release of tension, an uncontrollable giggle, a hysterical laugh that wouldn't stop until the tears came and poured down her face. She didn't try to wipe them away, she just sat there and let them cover her cheeks, tasting them as they fell onto her lips.

She could see Quincy's face through her tears, blurred and worried. She felt his hands on her arms.

"Abby," he said urgently, "stop it."

She gulped back her tears, her hysteria, and took a deep breath. "And then came the tornado," she said. "You must have been disappointed it didn't do more damage."

"No, of course not. I love this place."

"So much you'd do anything to get it back."

"Almost," he admitted, letting go of her and nervously shredding blades of grass with his fingers.

She drew in a ragged breath, the pain in her chest was almost unbearable. "So much you even tried to make me think you wanted me...at the pond, in the cellar." She stopped. She couldn't go on. Anything to get it back, even coming on to her.

"That had nothing to do with it," he said. "That was completely aside from everything else. I don't expect you to believe me after all this, Abby, but it's true. I didn't mean for that to happen. I wish it hadn't, but it did. It wasn't part of the plan."

"Then why...?" Her mind was spinning, trying to make sense of it all, or even part of it.

"Why? I don't know why. I don't need any more complications in my life. I've been burned once and so have you. But there's something between us. You know that. I could ask you the same question. Why?"

She shook her head. His voice was so distant, so detached, as if last night had happened to another person. He made her sound like a minor inconvenience while she was falling—yes, falling—in love with him. In love with a stranger—a stranger who was plotting to take her ranch away from her. She'd made mistakes before, but this was the worst, the crowning touch.

Why hadn't she suspected? Why hadn't she asked more questions? She'd been blinded, blinded by his looks, his kindness and his generosity, his willingness to work for nothing. She'd thought, because she'd made one big mistake before, that she was immune to making another. Instead she'd even topped the first. This time she'd lost her heart along with her ranch. She buried her face in her hands and sobbed.

"Abby." His voice broke. He reached for her. She felt his hand on her arm, his touch so warm, so gentle...so phony. She jumped to her feet and jammed her foot into the stirrup, swinging her leg over the back of the horse. Without looking at Quincy she took off down the hill at full speed, not knowing or caring where she was headed. All she knew was that she had to get away from him.

Quincy stood and watched her go. She was galloping full tilt toward the south pasture, crisscrossing the hill, letting the horse take her, her head bobbing up and down. He could picture her face streaked with tears and he felt as if his heart had been torn out of his chest. How could he have done it to her? How could he have hurt her so much, the one person he cared about more than anyone? The one person who'd trusted him, admired him, believed in him. *Damn.* He got on his horse and started after her. There was something he hadn't told her. It wouldn't make any difference to her now, but he had to say it, anyway.

She passed the long white fence that marked the bull pen and speeded up. He urged his horse on, narrowing the gap between them. He watched the gate swing open and he wondered why it was unlatched when the bull was inside. A wave of white-hot terror tore through him. Where was the bull? She continued to ride, unknowing, unseeing.

And then there he was, the bull with the Z cut into his horn, charging across the pasture toward her. Quincy screamed her name, but it was too late. The wind tore the scream from his throat. While he watched, the bull charged her horse. The horse reared and Abby flew in the air and then disappeared in the depths of the tall grass. The horse veered off to safety and the bull continued on his way to freedom.

When Quincy found her, she was lying pale and still in the grass. He vaulted off his horse and knelt down beside her. "Please, don't let her die," he kept repeating under his breath. "Let her live and I'll never ask for anything again. I'll give up the ranch and anything you want from me. *But don't let Abby die.*" He pressed his thumb to her wrist. Her pulse was weak but steady. Tears of relief coursed down his face. He lifted her in his arms and carried her back to the house. It took fifteen minutes and he prayed all the way.

She stirred in his arms. She had a cut over one eye and a mottled bruise on her temple. Other than that, he didn't know where she was hurt or how badly. He met Pop at the back door and told him to call the doctor. Pop's face went white and he disappeared. Quincy carried Abby to her bedroom and lay her on the bed. Her eyes were closed tightly and the marks where the tears had streaked down her face made stains on her pale cheeks.

He covered her with her comforter, and knelt on the floor with her hand held tightly in his, waiting for the doctor, waiting for her to come to. He was to blame for this, not the bull. He'd sent her off, blinded by tears, hurt and deceived. He couldn't believe what he'd done to get the ranch back. The ranch was nothing to him, nothing compared to Abby.

Chapter Ten

The doctor was tall and thin, with thick glasses. He was also younger than Quincy and said he was new in town. To Quincy he looked like a college student in his blue jeans and running shoes, his stethoscope hanging around his neck. While Quincy watched, he checked Abby's vital signs, cleaned and bandaged her head, measured the size of her pupils by shining a light into her eyes, and checked her reflexes and wiggled her toes. Then he put his instruments back into his bag.

"She's got a mild concussion, a brief loss of consciousness after a head injury. Usually happens after a car or motorcycle accident. In this case you say she was thrown by a horse?" he asked.

"Brief!" Quincy exclaimed. "She's been out for three-quarters of an hour!"

"She'll be coming around any minute. I don't think there's any internal bleeding and there shouldn't be any permanent damage. But we won't know for sure until after the next twenty-four to forty-eight hours. Right now it's best she stay put, but she'll need to be observed constantly during that time. Is there someone who can stay with her?"

"Me."

"You're her . . . ?"

"Partner." Quincy glanced down at Abby's pale face, half expecting her to object.

The doctor gave Quincy a long look, as if he were evaluating his ability to be an observer or a partner. Then he spoke. "All right. Here's what you need to look for. At first she'll be confused, may have some amnesia, drowsiness or delirium, but that should clear up in the next day or so. If it doesn't, I want to know about it, understand?"

Quincy nodded. Maybe she'd have just enough amnesia to forget what had happened and he could start all over.

"Oh, yes, she's got a couple of broken toes that just have to heal themselves. And they will as long as she stays off her feet. Got that?"

Quincy clenched his teeth together. Of course she had to stay off her feet. The doctor must be overworked and under a lot of stress, or else he knew that Quincy was to blame for this accident. He had never been treated like a half-witted moron before, not that he didn't deserve whatever punishment he got.

The doctor pulled the shades down to darken the room before he left. Pop appeared at the door, holding his hat in his hand. "She gonna be all right?" he asked in a whisper.

Quincy nodded. "She's got a concussion. The doc says she'll be coming around shortly and I've got to observe her for the next couple of days. She should be okay, but she's got to stay off her feet. She's got two broken toes."

"Amazing it ain't worse. What happened?"

Quincy explained about the bull, then he paused. "I, uh, told her the truth this morning. Who I was, why I came back. The whole thing."

"How'd she take it?"

Quincy looked at the dusty tips of his boots. "Not very well."

"I didn't expect she would. She was gettin' mighty fond of you."

Quincy jerked his head up and looked at Pop. "What makes you say that?"

"I got a sixth sense, like with the weather. It works with people, too. And I'm right about Abby. You must'uv broke her heart."

Quincy stared at him, feeling a chill creep through his bones. "I didn't mean to do that. She deserves better."

"Sure does. Maybe ya can make it up to her."

"By getting out of her life."

"Don't need to go to extremes," Pop cautioned. Then he took off to tell the boys to go find the bull and fetch the two horses before any more damage was done.

Quincy washed up in Abby's bathroom, then dragged the upholstered chair she kept in her room over to her bed and sat down on the edge of the cushion. He stared at the white bandage that crossed her forehead and matched the color of her skin. He swallowed nervously. Her eyelids fluttered and he leaned closer, willing her to open her eyes and look at him.

She raised her arm and reached for the bandage. Quincy caught her hand before she could touch it. She wrinkled her nose and winced.

"What . . . happened?" she mumbled, opening her eyes and squinting as if the sight of him hurt her eyes.

"The bull got out and charged Jessie this morning as you were riding by. You got thrown in the grass."

"Funny . . . I didn't see it," she said, then she pulled her hand from his and closed her eyes again. She fell asleep, or drifted off into unconsciousness, he didn't know which. But he was worried. How long was she supposed to be out and when should she stay awake? He wished he'd asked the doctor some questions. But the most important was the one only she could answer. Would she ever forgive him?

She moved restlessly, tossing and turning under the comforter. Quincy covered her with another blanket. The doctor had removed her blue jeans to examine her and had

unbuttoned her shirt to listen to her heart while Quincy
averted his eyes, but now he was afraid she was cold. He
wanted to put her nightgown on her. Getting up, he began
his search. In her dresser drawer he found a flannel granny
gown. When he returned to the bed, she was lying on her
side looking at him.

"How did I get here?" she whispered.

"I brought you."

"Thanks."

He smiled and heaved a sigh of relief, sitting back down.
She was clear, she was lucid, she was thanking him just like
she had before she found out. There was just one more
thing.

"Do you know who I am?" he asked.

She wrinkled her forehead and closed her eyes. Did that
mean she didn't recognize him or that she couldn't stand to
look at him? While he sat there watching her, with the
nightgown folded in his lap, Pop came back to report the
boys were still looking for the bull and that some group had
called wanting to come next week. The group who'd re-
cently canceled—the Sunday School Teachers.

"Guess we'll have to call 'em back and tell 'em Abby's out
for a good while."

"She'll be disappointed," Quincy said softly, his eyes on
her pale face. "Did you say 'teachers'?"

"Coming for a retreat."

"Seems to me we could handle a quiet bunch like Sunday school teachers," Quincy observed.

"Without Abby?" Pop asked.

"If we were to hire a cook."

"Like my cousin Lottie?" Pop asked.

Quincy nodded. Abby wouldn't like to be replaced in the
kitchen, but she wouldn't like to turn guests away, either.
And she wouldn't have to know that he was paying the cook.
They'd say Lottie was volunteering her time helping out
until Abby was well. He caught himself just in time. No.
He'd never lie to her again. Even if it was for her own good.

"You give her a call and I'll call the teachers and tell them to come ahead," Quincy said to Pop.

Pop tiptoed out and Quincy continued his vigil. At dinnertime, Pop took over and Quincy went down to the kitchen to find something to eat. He was stiff and sore, as if *he'd* been thrown from a horse, when it was only his psyche that had taken a beating. Before he went back upstairs, he squared things with the teachers. It was the least he could do. To get the guests coming back again before he took off for good.

He didn't expect Abby to be grateful for anything he did. In fact, she'd probably be mad as hell he'd taken matters into his own hands. But somebody had to make decisions until she was back to normal. If they'd been partners, he would have done it. He still thought it was a good idea. It could have worked. If things had been different. If he hadn't lied to her.

In the darkened bedroom, Abby rolled over onto her side and a stab of pain shot through her head. What was she doing in bed with the worst headache she'd ever had when she had so much work to do? She opened one eye and the room spun around. She closed her eye for a long moment, then tried again. She thought she saw Pop sleeping in the chair next to her bed. She had to be dreaming.

"Pop," she said hoarsely.

He jerked to attention.

"What happened?" she asked, closing her eyes. So it wasn't a dream.

"Ya got throwed off your horse. Yer hurt."

"No kidding." She fingered her bandage. "Quincy?" she said after a long moment.

"Want me to get him?" Pop jumped to his feet.

"No...no. Did you know...who he was?" she whispered.

"Yeah."

She squeezed her eyes shut and a tear trickled down the side of her face. It was all coming back, the lies, the deception. "He wants his ranch back."

"Ain't his anymore. It's yours, honey." Pop handed her a tissue.

She wiped her nose. It *was* hers, but what good did it do her? She couldn't manage it by herself, not financially, not emotionally. She couldn't even blow her nose by herself. Not today. She hadn't been able to manage her ranch before Quincy came, only she hadn't known it. She'd thought she was doing fine, but she hadn't known what fine was until he came. If he weren't so competent, so capable, so tough, so tender, so double-crossing— She closed her eyes to block out the thoughts of his betrayal.

"Anyway, he feels pretty bad about what he done," Pop said.

"Not as bad as I feel," she said, a wave of self-pity threatening to engulf her.

"Now wait just a minute," Pop said, leaning forward. "You got the ranch, he don't. He's been workin' pretty hard around here to help ya out."

She tried to raise her head, but she couldn't. "He tried to sabotage me. He turned off the pump and let it run dry. He let the bat loose in the bunkhouse. Did you know that?" she demanded with as much indignation as she could muster with the room spinning round.

Pop's face split into a crooked grin. "Nope, didn't know that. Well, it all backfired on him, didn't it? The way I look at it is ya got some free hard work out of him. Naturally he was hopin' to get the ranch back, but he didn't know how determined ya was to hang on. Naturally yer upset and yer feelin' poorly right now. But ya come out the long end of the deal, don'tcha think?"

Abby didn't answer. Pop's words blurred and ran together and she wasn't sure what he was talking about. She clutched the pillow to her cheek before she drifted off again, dreaming dreams of horses and cows and cowboys riding low in the saddle. In her dreams she felt Quincy's hands on her body, felt their warmth and gentleness as he undressed her. Her eyes flew open. This was no dream, he *was* undressing her. His fingers fumbled with the buttons of her shirt. Feebly she pushed his hands away.

"What are you doing?" she demanded shakily.

"I'm changing your clothes," Quincy said calmly. "So you'll be more comfortable. Here's your nightgown."

"I'll do it." She grabbed a handful of soft flannel and attempted to find the sleeves, but she couldn't even raise her arms to pull it over her head.

While she leaned back on her pillow watching helplessly, he continued to unbutton her shirt, then unclasp her bra, his fingers trembling just slightly. Then he lifted the nightgown over her head and worked her arms into the sleeves, slowly, carefully, until it settled around her waist. The soft fabric brushed against the sensitive tips of her breasts, causing a shudder to run through her.

Sitting on the edge of her bed, he drew the comforter up over her shoulders. "How do you feel?" he asked.

"Awful," she croaked. She probably looked awful, too. Besides awful, she felt bewildered, betrayed and ashamed. Little snippets of memory crept through the fog in her brain. So many clues, so obvious that he was not just a drifter. How could she have been so stupid?

"Hungry? Thirsty?"

She licked her dry lips. "A little."

He went to get a cup of tea, a can of ginger ale and a plate of toast. The doctor had left instructions on what she could eat and drink for the first few days. Three-course meals were not on the list.

As the memories of the past few weeks slowly sifted into her mind, she wanted to crawl under the covers and never come out. She sipped the soft drink he'd brought through a straw and looked at him over the rim of the can.

"You don't have to stay here with me."

"Yes I do. Doctor's orders."

"What's wrong with me?"

"Concussion, cuts, bruises and two broken toes."

And one broken heart. "Did he check my brain?"

Quincy hesitated. "Why?"

"Because I'm feeling awfully stupid."

His face reddened, but his gaze never left hers.

"Don't tell me you didn't notice," she said. "A person with normal intelligence would have figured out who you were. All it would've taken anyone else was one look at the way you and Magic reacted to each other that first day. Magic was your horse, always was, always had been. No wonder he didn't take to me or anyone else. He was waiting for you to come back." She pressed her free hand against her cheeks.

"Abby..."

"And the waitress, the whole town, *everybody* knew. Everybody but me. How do you think that makes me feel?"

"I know. I— What can I say? I'm sorry."

"Sorry?" Suddenly she was exhausted, emotionally, physically and mentally. She turned her back to him and closed her eyes.

"You have every right to be angry," he said.

"That's what Pop says," she said in a muffled voice.

"More than angry, furious."

When she got well she would have the energy to feel furious, but not now. She was too tired. All she felt was a deep sadness for what might have been. If he hadn't lied to her, if he'd been up-front about who he was and what he wanted....

She turned over to look at Quincy. "Pop says I won."

"He's right again."

"How do you figure?" she said, trying to focus on his face, the high cheekbones, the level gray gaze and the shock of hair that fell across his forehead.

"You've got the ranch, the will to make it go, and a great future ahead of you. What more do you want?"

She knew the answer to that question, she just couldn't say it. Couldn't say anything. Her lips were too dry, her eyelids too heavy to stay open any longer. She wanted more than that, yes. She wanted so much more. But she couldn't have it.

In the morning Pop was there with her breakfast, more tea and toast. With her head on the pillow, her eyes searched the room.

"He's outside takin' a break."

She felt the heat rise to her face and Pop grinned knowingly.

"I don't need somebody here all the time."

"That's what the doc said."

"I never even saw the doctor. How do I know he was here?"

"Who do you think bandaged ya up like a mummy, Quincy?"

"I wouldn't put it past him. He...he's done other things."

"I'll bet," Pop said, his eyes twinkling. "He didn't want to leave this mornin', but I put my foot down. He needed some space to shake off some of that guilt he's carrying around like a pack on his back."

"Because of me?"

"Who else?"

She flexed her good toes. "Tell him he doesn't have to feel guilty anymore. It's all over now."

"I reckon you'll tell him before he leaves."

Her heart skipped a beat and her breath caught in her throat. "He's leaving?"

"Of course."

"Of course," she repeated, looking out the window. What did she expect? Why should he stay? There was nothing for him here. She'd turned him down, turned down every proposal he'd made. And that was before she knew.

The sun poured in the window and as far as she could see were the hills and the tall grass. Off in the distance there was a man walking through the grass, his head held high. By his long strides, she knew it was Quincy, and her heart banged against her ribs. He loved this land so much, it must hurt him to think of leaving. And yet he *was* leaving. How could he stay? He wasn't meant to be anybody's hired hand. He was meant to be the boss. She'd known from the first minute she'd seen him as he'd come running up that hill that he was going to take charge.

"If ya don't mind," Pop said, getting to his feet, "I'll go downstairs a minute. Got a few things to do before tomorrow."

"Tomorrow?" She'd lost all track of time.

"When the new group comes in."

She forced herself to think. How could she not remember what group was coming? Maybe she had amnesia or maybe even brain damage. "I can't remember..." she confessed.

"Ya can't remember because ya was asleep when they called, but me and Quincy, we handled it. They're just a bunch of teachers, Sunday school teachers, who won't bother ya while you're gettin' well. We made sure of that."

"But who's going to cook for them?"

"My cousin Lottie I spoke to ya about. She's goin' to help out for a while till yer back on yer feet."

"Really?" Abby felt weak and helpless and unneeded. So the ranch was running without her. Without her, a new group had been scheduled and a new cook had been hired. With what money? "Go," she instructed Pop. "I'll be fine."

The Sunday School Teachers group came. She heard them in the dining room and saw them from the window. She wanted to show them the calves and chickens, she wanted to lecture them on the ecology of the tall grass, but she could only lie there day after day and watch them walk down the path beneath her window.

Quincy came and told her how much they liked the place. Pop came and brought her dinner. Pot roast and potato pancakes one night, corned beef and cabbage the next. She wasn't bad, that Lottie. Someday, if she could afford it, Abby might hire a cook to help out. But right now she wanted to get up, get out of bed. She was tired of this room, tired of wearing a nightgown and a bandage.

Her eye on the bathroom door, she eased herself to the floor with a thump and braced her hands against the carpet, the shock setting off waves of pain through her body. The door opened and she found herself looking straight at Quincy's boots.

"Where do you think you're going?" he asked.

"To the bathroom to wash my hair." She'd had enough of being taken care of. Enough of being treated like an invalid. It was tiring. It was demeaning.

"No you're not."

"To take a bath, then."

"Okay. Stay here while I fill the tub."

She leaned back against the side of the bed, her head cushioned on the quilt, and watched him go.

He was back in a few minutes. "Take off your clothes and I'll lift you in the tub."

"*What?*"

"You heard me," he said gruffly. "It's not as if I haven't seen you without your clothes before."

"All of them?" she asked incredulously.

"Do you want a bath or not?"

"Yes."

"Do you want your toes to heal?"

"Of course. But will you close your eyes?"

"Sure."

She hesitated before she slowly and painfully pulled her nightgown over her head. She knew he was a practiced liar and yet she wanted a bath very badly. Tossing her nightgown onto the bed, she closed her eyes as if that would prevent him from seeing her. Lifting her arms slightly, she told him she was ready. She felt his hands on her, strong and firm, then his shirt was against her breasts, his arm around her bare bottom. She shivered and he pressed her close, so close she was in danger of losing herself in his arms.

She buried her face against his chest and he stifled a moan deep in his chest. She heard it and felt a fire start deep in her being. The next thing she knew she was being gently lowered into the warm water. When she opened her eyes, he was gone and she was immersed in fragrant bubbles. Carefully, she stretched her legs out in front of her and, keeping her one bandaged foot on the edge, she let herself sink down until only her head was above water. Slowly the tension left her muscles. Gradually she felt her body become weightless, suspended in the elements.

"Quincy?" she called.

"Uh-huh." His voice was just outside the door.

"This feels wonderful."

"I know."

"This was your tub, wasn't it?"

"Yep. I ordered the extra long." Quincy leaned against the bathroom door, his legs too weak to hold him up. He'd seen her naked body once before today, but this was different. Carrying her, feeling her soft skin with his hands, had sent white-hot desire shooting through him. How much more could a man take? He was supposed to feel nothing but guilt, but there was more, so much more.

If he could just get through the week, get her on her feet again, send the guests off with happy memories the way she would have done, then he could leave and know that things would go on without him. There might be an occasional moment when she'd miss an extra hand for branding or calving, but on the whole he suspected he hadn't made much of a dent in her life while he'd been there.

He heard her splashing and he pictured bubbles cascading over her shoulders, tiny droplets of water trickling down her full breasts, imagined the heat turning her skin the color of rose petals. Perspiration broke out on his forehead.

"Quincy?"

He pressed his ear against the door. "What?"

"Do you think Lottie's a better cook than I am?"

He smiled to himself. "Not better, just different."

"It might be nice to have some help in the kitchen, someday."

"It's something to think about," he said cautiously. It was a good sign, her thinking of the future, of expanding, succeeding. "One thing," he continued. "I bet she couldn't put together a picnic lunch like yours—chicken salad, asparagus and white wine.''

"I had too much wine that day," she mused. "I asked you what you were doing. You said you were along for the ride. I should have known then."

"I lied to you," he said. He pressed his shoulder blades against the door. "I've lied to you from the first day I got here." This was not the way to apologize to her, but it was a start, and it couldn't be avoided any longer. "I'm sorry."

There was a long silence. If only she'd say something, anything. He didn't expect her to forgive him. Why should she? She had a right to be angry. He *expected* her to be angry, even furious. But he hadn't expected her to be silent. It wasn't like her. Had she fallen asleep and slipped under the water and drowned?

"Abby?" he called out frantically.

"Yes?"

Thank God, she was still alive. "Still want your hair washed?"

"I can't lift my arms."

"I'll do it for you." He pushed the door open a crack. If she objected, he'd back out. All he could see of her was the back of her head. Her blond hair curled in tendrils down the back of her neck, but her body was completely submerged.

"Okay," she said languidly, as if the heat had drained what little energy she had.

He moved closer and kneeled on the floor, a puddle of water soaking the knees of his jeans. He poured a glob of rose-scented shampoo into his hand and worked it into her hair, massaging carefully around her bandage, around the cut in her forehead. She tilted her head back against the porcelain and sighed deeply.

"Feel good?" he murmured against her temple.

"Mmm."

He twisted her hair into a spiral and continued to rub her scalp with a firm, rotating motion, his fingers moving to the back of her neck and the sensitive spot behind her ears, using the shampoo as a lubricant, as an excuse to touch her.

Abby felt her bones melt, her body turn to jelly, as Quincy continued to mold her into whatever he wanted. If she had the energy she'd get out of the water and fling herself at him, or pull him into the water with her. No matter what he'd done, he had the power to make her forget, to fill her mind with him and only him, his scent, his touch, his mouth, his skin.

He made her feel so relaxed, yet at the same time so alive every nerve ending was tingling with anticipation. Of what? It was over between them. Whatever had been there was based on a false premise, that he was there to help her. Now that she knew the truth about him she could not—*would* not—let herself get carried away by the magic in his hands. She'd tell him to stop. She'd tell him she felt nothing for him. In a few minutes. Just a few minutes.

But he stopped washing her hair before she had a chance to tell him. He rinsed it with the use of a plastic cup and then he took a towel and wrapped it around her head. She laid her head back and closed her eyes. He pulled the plug and when the water spiraled down the drain he picked her up and wrapped her whole body in a gigantic bath towel, carrying her back to bed.

She forgot to tell him not to look. It didn't matter. Nothing mattered but the way he made her feel—warm, safe, protected, cared for. She snuggled back into her bed, the towel still wrapped around her body, the comforter a soft cloud on top of her, and she slept. A long, healing, dreamless sleep.

Quincy watched her eyes drift closed and he tenderly unwrapped the towel from around her head. He touched her lips with his fingers and then traced the curve of her cheek. Then he settled back into the chair to watch her sleep, wishing he had the nerve to tell her he loved her, just once before he left. But what good would it do? She wouldn't believe him.

The doctor came back the next day and replaced the large bandage with a smaller one. He told her she could get up and even go downstairs if someone carried her. He told her to expect to be moody, depressed, have headaches and personality changes as a result of her concussion, but they wouldn't last. Her toes were healing nicely and soon she could get around on her own again.

The day after that she sat in the parlor on the chintz-covered couch, unable to look in the direction of the desk with the piles of bills just where she'd left them before the accident. The last time she was there was the day Quincy had offered to buy half the ranch from her and be her partner. What if she'd said yes? What if she'd accepted and then found out who he was? Would she feel any worse than she did now? *Could* she feel any worse than she did now?

Was his offer sincere, or was it just another trick like letting the bat loose? She'd never know and she didn't really *want* to know. She stared out the window. The guests had left yesterday and Pop and Quincy had lined up still another group for tomorrow. The Friends of the Prairie, who had canceled earlier, were coming at last.

It was quiet, except for the buzzing of a bee just outside the window. As far as she could see was the land she loved so much, the wide blue sky and the endless prairie. It was a big ranch. Too big for one person. Too much for one person to handle. She'd denied it before, but she couldn't deny it any longer. She needed a partner, but it was too late. Quincy was leaving, and Quincy was not a man to change his mind.

As if she'd made him appear by thinking of him, Quincy materialized outside the open window.

"How're you feeling?" he asked, wiping his forehead with a bandanna. She had to shade her eyes to look at him with the brilliant sunshine behind him.

"Fine. I miss being outside, miss riding, cooking..."

"It won't be long. The doc says you're almost ready to get back on your feet. Mind if I come in for a minute?"

She shook her head. He sounded so formal, so polite. He came through the front door wearing a clean shirt and jeans.

A cold, icy fear gripped her and she wedged her spine against the back of the couch.

He braced his arms against the door frame. "I came to say goodbye."

Her heart stopped. "For good?" She pressed her hands together to keep from shaking uncontrollably.

"Oh, I don't know about that. How can you say anything's for good?"

He stuffed his hands into his back pockets so casually she wanted to scream, *How can you go? How can you leave? Don't you care about the ranch, about me?*

"But first I want to apologize. I— You don't know how sorry I am I lied to you. I never meant to hurt you. I never meant to fall..." He clenched his hands into fists and stopped abruptly. If she didn't know better she would have sworn he was close to tears. But he couldn't be. Cowboys didn't cry. Everyone knew that.

She stared at him, her eyes wide, feeling the tears prick her eyelids. "It's all right," she blurted out. "I understand how you feel about the land. If someone had taken it away from me I might have done the same... but..." Oh, no, she was going to cry and spoil it all. If he was leaving, she didn't want his last view of her to be with tears in her eyes. She wanted him to remember her being strong, capable, confident.

"I'll miss you," she said. Miss him? The way she'd miss the sun and the moon if they left.

He shook his head. "You'll be fine. You're strong, you've got what it takes. You know that first day I saw you...?"

"When you unloaded the truck for me?"

"I thought you were a fragile hothouse flower, out of place here on the ranch. But now I see you're like prairie larkspur, you bounce back even after you've been trampled."

The words embedded themselves in her mind and touched her deeply. "You really think so?"

"I know so." His eyes warmed to the color of smoke from a lazy bonfire on a fall day and made her face flush.

"What about your offer to buy half the ranch?" she asked anxiously.

"I think after what's happened you can consider it null and void, obviously."

"Obviously," she repeated numbly. "It's none of my business, but where are you going?"

"I'm not sure."

"I thought you loved it here."

"I did."

He didn't say, *But I don't anymore.* He didn't have to. If he couldn't have it all, he didn't want any part of it. She understood that. He didn't have to spell it out for her. So why didn't she let him go since he so obviously wanted to go? She just kept feeling that if she said the right thing he'd stay. Only she didn't know what that was. She'd tried everything.

"Quincy? You said I'd be fine. I . . . I feel the same way about you. You'll be fine, too. Whatever you do, wherever you go."

"Think so?" A faint, ironic smile crossed his face.

"I don't think you're as cynical as you used to be, not about women, anyway."

"Maybe not. Anyway, I'm glad I could help out a little."

"A lot."

He gave her a crooked smile and backed out the door. She leaned forward, a lump in her throat the size of a thistle and twice as sharp. She heard his footsteps on the stairs, his boots crunch the gravel on the driveway, and then, in the distance, she heard his truck start up. She couldn't breathe, couldn't speak, couldn't call his name and tell him to come back. Suddenly she knew what she had to do. Staggering to her feet, she hobbled to the front porch, her toes throbbing in protest.

She stumbled down the driveway and around the side of the barn and flung herself against the door of his truck, the tears streaming down her face. The motor was running and he had been about to pull away, but if he was leaving, then she was leaving, too. The ranch without him was worthless.

He opened the door and with one arm he swung her up onto his lap.

She threw her arms around his neck and hugged him so tightly he couldn't speak if he'd wanted to.

"You forgot something," she said between sobs.

"What's that?" His tears mingled with hers.

"Me."

"Oh, God, Abby. I couldn't leave you. I might have gotten as far as Emporia, but I would have come back. I would have begged you to take me back as something—anything."

"Even a partner... or a—a husband?"

He held her by the shoulders and looked into her glistening blue eyes. "Is that what you want, a partner or a husband?"

"I want *you*. I love you."

"You've got me." He reached for the ignition and turned off the engine. "Until the well runs dry and the cows come home. Forever."

The soft muted sounds of cattle mooing caused her to look out the passenger window. "Speaking of cows..." Several cows had ambled toward the truck, curious and round-eyed, and were pressing themselves against the door.

Quincy followed her gaze. "It's sure hard to get anything done when you're trapped inside your truck by a herd of cows."

"I don't know," she said, ignoring the steering wheel pressing into her back. "What do you *want* to do?"

He ran his hand along the curve of her cheek and tilted her chin to cover her lips with his. And with that kiss he answered all her questions, forever.

*   *   *   *   *

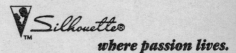

MILLION DOLLAR SWEEPSTAKES (III)

No purchase necessary. To enter, follow the directions published. Method of entry may vary. For eligibility, entries must be received no later than March 31, 1996. No liability is assumed for printing errors, lost, late or misdirected entries. Odds of winning are determined by the number of eligible entries distributed and received. Prizewinners will be determined no later than June 30, 1996.

Sweepstakes open to residents of the U.S. (except Puerto Rico), Canada, Europe and Taiwan who are 18 years of age or older. All applicable laws and regulations apply. Sweepstakes offer void wherever prohibited by law. Values of all prizes are in U.S. currency. This sweepstakes is presented by Torstar Corp., its subsidiaries and affiliates, in conjunction with book, merchandise and/or product offerings. For a copy of the Official Rules send a self-addressed, stamped envelope (WA residents need not affix return postage) to: MILLION DOLLAR SWEEPSTAKES (III) Rules, P.O. Box 4573, Blair, NE 68009, USA.

EXTRA BONUS PRIZE DRAWING

No purchase necessary. The Extra Bonus Prize will be awarded in a random drawing to be conducted no later than 5/30/96 from among all entries received. To qualify, entries must be received by 3/31/96 and comply with published directions. Drawing open to residents of the U.S. (except Puerto Rico), Canada, Europe and Taiwan who are 18 years of age or older. All applicable laws and regulations apply; offer void wherever prohibited by law. Odds of winning are dependent upon number of eligible entries received. Prize is valued in U.S. currency. The offer is presented by Torstar Corp., its subsidiaries and affiliates in conjunction with book, merchandise and/or product offering. For a copy of the Official Rules governing this sweepstakes, send a self-addressed, stamped envelope (WA residents need not affix return postage) to: Extra Bonus Prize Drawing Rules, P.O. Box 4590, Blair, NE 68009, USA.

SWP-S594

IT'S OUR 1000TH SILHOUETTE ROMANCE,
AND WE'RE CELEBRATING!

JOIN US FOR A SPECIAL COLLECTION OF LOVE STORIES
BY AUTHORS YOU'VE LOVED FOR YEARS, AND
NEW FAVORITES YOU'VE JUST DISCOVERED.
JOIN THE CELEBRATION...

SILHOUETTE ROMANCE...VIBRANT, FUN AND EMOTIONALLY
RICH! TAKE ANOTHER LOOK AT US! AND AS PART OF THE
CELEBRATION, READERS CAN RECEIVE A FREE GIFT!

YOU'LL FALL IN LOVE ALL OVER
AGAIN WITH
SILHOUETTE ROMANCE!

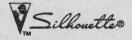

CEL1000

Get set for an exciting new series from
bestselling author

ELIZABETH AUGUST

Join us for the first book:

THE FORGOTTEN HUSBAND

Amnesia kept Eloise from knowing the real reason she'd
married cold, distant Jonah Tavish. But brief moments of sweet
passion kept her searching for the truth. Can anyone help Eloise
and Jonah rediscover love?

Meet Sarah Orman in *WHERE THE HEART IS.* She has a way
of showing up just when people need them most. And with her
wit and down-to-earth charm, she brings couples together—
for keeps.

Available in July, only from

Silhouette
R O M A N C E™

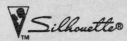

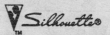

CELEBRATION 1000! Free Gift Offer

ORDER INFORMATION:

To receive your free AUSTRIAN CRYSTAL BRACELET, send three original proof-of-purchase coupons from any SILHOUETTE ROMANCE™ title published in April through July 1994 with the Free Gift Certificate completed, plus $1.75 for postage and handling (check or money order—please do not send cash) payable to Silhouette Books CELEBRATION 1000! Offer. Hurry! Quantities are limited.

FREE GIFT CERTIFICATE   096 KBM

Name:_____

Address:_____

City:_____ State/Prov.:_____ Zip/Postal:_____

Mail this certificate, three proofs-of-purchase and check or money order to CELEBRATION 1000! Offer, Silhouette Books, 3010 Walden Avenue, P.O. Box 9057, Buffalo, NY 14269-9057 or P.O. Box 622, Fort Erie, Ontario L2A 5X3. Please allow 4-6 weeks for delivery. Offer expires August 31, 1994.

PLUS

Every time you submit a completed certificate with the correct number of proofs-of-purchase, you are automatically entered in our CELEBRATION 1000! SWEEPSTAKES to win the GRAND PRIZE of $1000 CASH! PLUS, 1000 runner-up prizes of a FREE Silhouette Romance™, autographed by one of CELEBRATION 1000!'s special featured authors, will be awarded. No purchase or obligation necessary to enter. See below for alternate means of entry and how to obtain complete sweepstakes rules.

CELEBRATION 1000! SWEEPSTAKES
NO PURCHASE OR OBLIGATION NECESSARY TO ENTER

You may enter the sweepstakes without taking advantage of the CELEBRATION 1000! FREE GIFT OFFER by hand-printing on a 3" x 5" card (mechanical reproductions are not acceptable) your name and address and mailing it to: CELEBRATION 1000! Sweepstakes, P.O. Box 9057, Buffalo, NY 14269-9057 or P.O. Box 622, Fort Erie, Ontario L2A 5X3. Limit: one entry per envelope. Entries must be sent via First Class mail and be received no later than August 31, 1994. No liability is assumed for lost, late or misdirected mail.

Sweepstakes is open to residents of the U.S. (except Puerto Rico) and Canada, 18 years of age or older. All federal, state, provincial, municipal and local laws apply. Offer void wherever prohibited by law. Odds of winning dependent on the number of entries received. For complete rules, send a self-addressed, stamped envelope to: CELEBRATION 1000! Rules, P.O. Box 4200, Blair, NE 68009.

 ONE PROOF OF PURCHASE

096KBM

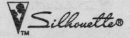